The Blinks

'Anger'

By Andrea Chatten

Illustrations by Rachel Pesterfield

First published in 2015 by

The Solopreneur Publishing Company Ltd

Cedars Business Centre, Barnsley Road, Hemsworth, West Yorkshire WF9 4PU

www.thesolopreneur.co.uk

ISBN 978-0-9934527-0-3

Printed in the U.K.

For further copies, and other titles in the series, please go to - www.oodlebooks.com. Also available on Amazon and Kindle.

Dedication

This book is dedicated to my wonderful husband Simon, my Mum & Uncle Peter & Auntie Karin, for your permanent support.

Contents

Chapter 1

Robbie

This is Robbie.

Robbie is 10 years old and lives with his Mum, and his four brothers and sisters in a Northern City which you might or might not have heard of, called Sheffoold. Robbie is the second eldest child in his family, but since the death of his Dad, when he was 7, he has had to work much harder with his older sister to try and fill the space that his Dad left.

This has left Robbie with a lot of sadness and other feelings that Robbie doesn't like, which I am sure you can understand. However, recently Robbie has noticed that he feels angry too quickly, for too long and too often and it is starting to become a problem.

Robbie's house can only be described as chaotic. With 6 of them squeezed into a three bedroomed semi-detached house, there isn't room to swing a cat (which Robbie has never tried to do, ever. Not even when he was three years old and was being curious as to how strong cats tails were!!!)

Poor Mrs Tucker struggles every day to try and bring about some sense of order, but with five children, two dogs, a cat, a guinea pig and two dwarf hamsters, order sadly falls by the wayside. It wasn't always as hard as this.

When Mr Tucker was around things ran smoother, for the majority of the time anyway. That was until Dad had one of his moody days and then things became more difficult. Dad's anger on these days could cause the whole day to change. Mrs Tucker tried her best at being a working mum and wife and in fact, you could say that as Mums go, she was 'on it'. However, that also changed after Mr Tucker died.

Mrs Tucker had pretty much been sad and lonely ever since that dreadful day and was also becoming moodier and angrier because life had become so hard.

Robbie lived at the heart of this sad, angry world. Although he did his best to try to hang on to his happiness, he found himself feeling sadder and angrier on a daily basis. This was why Robbie enjoyed going to school. There, he was surrounded by lots of people who he liked and who liked him. More than that, he enjoyed being part of a world that felt fun, where his worries and anger didn't seem too intense.

Amanda had always been his best friend, for as long as he could remember. He remembers with a smile how they used to play all day together at the nursery, usually out on the pedal cars, or in the sandpit. Robbie often wondered if Amanda realised just how good a friend she was to him. He did always make sure that Amanda was the very first person who saw a well-practised diablo trick, which to him was a true act of friendship.

So Robbie used to spend most of his days at school trying to cram in as much fun as possible, before going home to a very different world. Very few happy times had happened there over the last few years.

Home had become a difficult place to be. It had never been easy, but it had now become filled with difficult people and difficult times. Home made Robbie feel sad. The longer he felt sad, the easier it was to become angry when things didn't go how they should have done. However, every time Robbie got angry, the less he liked himself. The less he liked himself, the more of a failure he felt. The more of a failure he felt, the sadder he got. The sadder he got, the angrier he became and so it went on and on....

Amanda was one of the people in school who had noticed Robbie's behaviour had changed over the last few months, and that it was, perhaps, becoming a bigger problem. However no one could ignore what happened on that Tuesday morning just before register.

Just to set the scene and to help you understand just how poor Robbie was feeling, you need to know a few things. From Robbie coming home from school last night, until leaving for school this morning, everything had been chaos for Robbie and his family, times by ten! Even for the Tucker household this chaos could be classed as off the scale for disastrous events. This is the series of events that happened within the four walls of 15 Woodstock Road.

Monday 4pm onwards:

1. Dusty the guinea pig died.

2. Mrs Tucker was recovering from the flu, so had spent all day in bed and had not been shopping or cooked anything hot for tea for three days.

3. Vanessa (Robbie's older sister – age 14) had an exam the next day so was highly stressed and needed to revise.

4. There had been a power cut so the house had no electricity, or internet (revision nightmare!).

5. Beth (Robbie's younger sister, and

one of the triplets – age 8) had fallen off the climbing frame at school and badly twisted her ankle.

6. Robbie, Charlie & Lex (Robbie's younger brothers and the other two triplets) went to the shop to buy bread and baked beans for tea and lost the £5 note on the way!

7. Due to the power cut and lost £5, everyone had to have cold hotdog sausages, cold sweetcorn and peas for tea, followed by breakfast cereal for pudding (with rationed milk nevertheless!).

8. The triplets were hungry, ratty and annoying.

9. Vanessa spent most of the night crying because she couldn't concentrate on her revision and had no access to the internet for her Teenogram app to enjoy as a reward.

10. Mrs Tucker shouted at everyone

between coughs and splutters and because she felt so ill, everything was a chore. And to top it all no-one had saved her a hot dog sausage.

11. They buried Dusty in the garden.

12. Robbie didn't sleep very well as Charlie & Lex were coughing and sniffing all night, coming down with Mum's flu.

Tuesday 7 am onwards:

1. All the contents of the freezer had defrosted due to the power cut.

2. Everyone had to have fish fingers, hash browns, profiteroles, and strawberry cheesecake for breakfast!

3. Vanessa's hair straighteners broke, so she had a total teenage strop and broke a cup.

4. Beth cut her foot on the broken cup,

so blood was trailed through the whole house.

5. Lex & Charlie now had the flu.
6. Mum had to be off work again to look after the boys, even though it was the first day that she was due back to the surgery.
7. It would have been Dad's 45th birthday.

Robbie left the house that Tuesday morning feeling stressed, tense and on the verge of tears, but at the same time he felt a huge sense of relief. He was about to escape the most hectic twenty-four hours he had ever recalled. Today could only be better, couldn't it? Unfortunately, Robbie didn't leave the hectic events behind him at all.

All the way to school Robbie was replaying the sequence of events in his head and the more he did, the angrier he got. He then found himself bombarded with sad thoughts that sounded like a conversation in his head:

"Why does this always happen to me?" said Robbie.

"Because your life is a mess," he replied.

"Yeah, and you have the most annoying family in the world," agreed Robbie.

"My life makes me so mad. I'm really, really angry!" he ranted.

"And, it's Dad's birthday today. He should be here making the day okay. All the family should be looking forward to going out for tea later and having some birthday cake," interrupted Robbie.

"Today is going to be rubbish and I hate everything!" he bellowed from deep inside his thoughts.

Just as Robbie finished the angry conversation in his head, he found himself at school. By this point Robbie had convinced himself that today was going to be a rubbish day, so all of his joy and hope for a good day had slowly disappeared. Sadly he was not wrong.

Chapter 2

Pencil Shavings

As Robbie approached the school gates, he felt like he had a ball of fire brewing in his tummy. He had never felt this sensation so strongly before and he wasn't sure he liked it. He scanned the playground desperate to find Amanda, knowing that she would provide the calm he needed to help change his angry feelings.

The longer Robbie searched in desperation for Amanda the more frustrated he became. Where was she? He then found himself getting angry at Amanda for not being there when he needed her, even though poor Amanda hadn't done anything wrong.

Just as Robbie was about to go and find someone else to stand with he heard Amanda's laugh coming from the covered seated area, by the toilets. Oh thank goodness, thought Robbie, she is here. At last I can be with someone who will make me feel better.

What Robbie hadn't realised was that Amanda, Asif, Erin & Jamie had been secretly planning a way of having some fun with Robbie to make him feel special and important. They had all noticed that he seemed sadder and more grumpy recently and it was agreed that Robbie, who they knew had an ace sense of humour, would love the attention of his best friends. How wrong could they have been?

As Robbie walked past the hedge, he saw all of his closest friends laughing and joking. He wanted to know what could have been so funny, in hope that they would share it with him quickly, as he was desperate for a laugh. However when Robbie appeared, everyone stopped talking, stopped laughing and looked shocked that Robbie was stood there in front of them.

"Hi Robbie," spluttered Amanda, in a higher pitch than normal.

This instantly made Robbie feel uncomfortable.

"What were you all laughing at?" asked Robbie, knowing perfectly well that they were laughing at him.

"Erm, it's erm, you know, erm nothing really," interjected Erin, who was a new member of the friendship group.

In about two seconds flat, Robbie decided that he no longer liked Erin, because that was the fakest and most rubbish response he had ever heard. Maybe she was turning the whole group against him. The fireball in Robbie's tummy started spitting such angry feelings that he could feel them moving across his body. His fists started to clench, his breathing speeded up and he could feel his legs starting to stiffen.

He felt his muscles tighten. He noticed his face getting red. He also felt the anger lava from deep in his belly, reach his chest because his heart was pounding faster than ever before.

Robbie then did something that he was starting to do more often, and that was letting his angry feelings lead him to do bad things. Without any feelings of control, he shoved Erin on the shoulder, in a way that made the rest of the group jump up in horror.

"Robbie, what are you doing? That was out of order. Erin didn't deserve that," shouted Amanda. She put her arm around Erin, who was obviously upset.

This hurt Robbie even more. Why was Amanda not putting her arm around him, when he so desperately needed it?

"Go away all of you, I hate you," bellowed Robbie.

With this, he stomped inside, slammed the door and headed for the toilets, feeling like he was about to cry. As he sat thinking in one of the cubicles, tears started rolling down his cheeks. Amanda had obviously found a new friend in Erin and she was turning everyone against him. Out of all of the things that had happened in the last twenty four hours, this thought made Robbie feel the saddest.

Why today of all days? How had he not noticed it until now?

Back in the playground Amanda, Asif, Erin & Jamie also tried to get their heads around what had just happened, unsure why Robbie had just been so mean to them all.

At 8.50am, the bell at Croft House Primary School rang for everyone to start going into their classrooms. Robbie left the toilets at lightning speed. He quickly splashed water on his eyes to try and cover up redness left by the tears. He needed to be in the classroom first. He wanted to bury his head in his book and hope that no-one noticed him or said anything to him at all.

As the rest of the class entered the room, Mrs Jackson pottered around getting things ready for the day ahead. Robbie knew his teacher had noticed him come in first because she said hello, but why hadn't she checked in with him, in case he needed help?

This also revved up Robbie's inner volcano and he found that he had begun criticising himself. Robbie's negative thoughts chattered away with endless unkind things about himself. Thoughts about him being a horrible person, no-one liking him, and that he suddenly hated everyone. Each one of these thoughts sent hot angry fire into his blood which made his cheeks turn redder and his mouth feel dry. But still he tried to hide away, so he sank deeper in to his chair wanting to become small and invisible. This was never going to happen when the person who sits next to you is Ben!

Ben was taller than most of his year group and hadn't mastered the art of being controlled or gentle. He bounded around like a puppy. This made him a great addition to any team sport that you were playing, as his energy and power got results. However in a confined space, with twenty-nine other children, Ben was like a tornado!

Robbie heard Ben before he saw him and found himself peering above his book. As Ben entered, things started flying with his larger than life physical movements. Poor Esther was accidentally banged on the head with his bag. Matt's spelling log was knocked off a table and trampled on. But what was heading closer and closer to Robbie could push him over the edge.

"Ben, Ben, BEN!" shouted Mrs Jackson. "Slow down and please be careful how you're moving around the classroom. Someone is going to get hurt."

Although Mrs Jackson was making every attempt to reduce any further damage, it, unfortunately, had the opposite effect. As Ben made an emergency stop, he went over on his ankle which caused him to stumble right onto Robbie, who ended up falling off his chair, taking the contents of the table with him. That was the final straw for Robbie, the inner fireball exploded.

He picked up the table box and threw it directly at Ben who was lying, shell shocked, on the floor. But what Robbie did next was far worse. He picked up the pencil sharpening pot which had not been emptied for a very long time, and deliberately tipped the entire contents of the pot all over Ben's head!

Everything went still.

The room gasped in shock.

Mrs Jackson was lost for words.

Poor Ben was frantically trying to shake off the debris before it got into his eyes, nose and mouth.

Robbie ran out of the class and hid in the cloakroom.

Robbie could hear Mrs Jackson take control of the class by telling them all to be seated and to read quietly. She asked Daisy & Albie to pick out the remaining pencil shavings from Ben's hair and tidy him up. Then Robbie heard her footsteps coming towards the cloakroom.

Robbie had buried himself deep under the coats, feeling ashamed and embarrassed and repeatedly punched himself on the leg.

"Robbie Tucker, get out of those coats immediately and come here. What you've just done is very serious and I too am very cross," said Mrs Jackson, raising her voice.

The whole of class Y6J were quieter than sleeping snails, straining to hear what was happening in the cloakroom.

Amanda suddenly felt worried about her friend. Although Robbie had been a bit edgy recently, he had never ever been aggressive or violent. She then thought about what they had done earlier. From the cloakroom, another kerfuffle was heard with Mrs Jackson shouting again.

"Right, if you don't come out of there by the count of five, then you'll be going to Mr Mosely's office and I will be arranging a meeting with your Mum. One, two, three..." ordered Mrs Jackson.

No way could Robbie handle being shouted at again by Mrs Jackson or Mr Mosely, the Deputy Headteacher. So he picked himself up, ran out of the cloakroom, sending Mrs Jackson flying as he did, through the school and out of reception. He didn't stop until he found himself standing on the front step of his house, panting, hot, teary and scared.

But what was he going to do now?

Chapter 3

Baffled by a button in the Bakery!

Rosie, the fabulous owner of the local bakery always worked hard cleaning down the shop making sure that everything was spick and span, ready for her returning at 3 am. Tonight, though, something had caused her to stop for a moment.

As Rosie took hold of the iced doughnut tray, she noticed something glistening in the corner of it. At first she was going to tip it, with the other sugar strands, into the bin, but this item was different and it made her pause. On closer inspection, Rosie felt sure that it was a tiny button.

Yes, it was definitely a red glittery button.

However, what baffled Rosie was that this button was tiny; way too small for any human clothing, in fact too small for any dolls' clothing (It was probably no bigger than this letter 'o'). How could a tiny, red, glittery button be there amongst the doughnut sugar strands?

At that moment, Rosie remembered the story of The Elves and The Shoemaker, a favourite from when she was a child, and she smile. Rosie's imagination ran wild in the fields of her childhood. For a short moment, instead of a shoemaker, she was the baker character in the book and she had precious little friends who visited her at night.

A chuckle erupted from Rosie's mouth which jolted her back to the present moment and the realisation that more cleaning still needed to be done. Rosie popped the button into a small piece of kitchen paper and slipped it into her pocket. She already loved the little button for making her feel young again and that made it more special.

Rosie had no idea how close to reality she was with what she had just discovered. Little did she know that her bakery, in the heart of Sheffoold, was the specially selected midnight venue used every night by some very special souls called The Blinks!

The button did, in fact, belong to Blink 28271 - Peter Practise!

At the sugar dough buffet the evening before, Peter Practise had removed his hat to inspect its quality. He'd had this hat for a long, long time. He started wondering whether he might treat himself to a new one when he completed the project he was currently working on.

Without realising, Peter Practise had been accidently sitting on the button, causing it to snap off as he lifted his hat to his head. Unfortunately due to the tray being crammed with celebrating Blinks enjoying the feast, he was unable to find and store the button to replace it later. He had hoped that by making a special effort to get to the bakery early the next night, he might be reunited with his shiny red hat button, which he was now missing dreadfully.

The Blinks, as you can imagine, are very busy every day, searching for children and young people who are having difficult times. Their whole purpose is to share the love and wisdom of the many wonderful people who have contributed to their creation.

The Universe, you see, is full of tiny little fluff balls that are the departing gifts as people pass from this world to whatever is next. When 419 speckles of goodness have formed together, the 420th injects something amazing and a Blink is created!

Each Blink has a number which many suggest relates to their number in the sequence of Blink formation. Many of the wise ones have lower numbers which not only reflect their age, but also experience and knowledge, for the other Blinks to learn from.

The Blinks are all very different. Some change colour as they evolve, showing that they have gained skills in certain things.

Some are multicoloured showing their all rounded learning and development. Needless to say, all Blinks are good hearted and committed to making children feel as happy as possible.

This is why The Blinks meet every midnight, in a bakery, in every City across the world. The meeting is the time when new children are brought to the attention of Chief Blink and her panel. It is also when all Blinks take part in the 'Five Stages' of Blinkery.

Stage 1...***On the lookout!*** This stage involves finding the kids who are not dealing with life very well. The Blinks involved at this stage are either still in the research part, trying to find the right child, or are close to selecting a person who they feel needs urgent Blink wisdom.

The empty chocolate éclair trays, which sit in the main display cabinet just in front of the till, have become the meeting place for all Stage 1 Blinks. This is where they chat about the possible children who could become new projects.

Not all Blinks have such an eventful day and so get together creating the sugar dough buffet. This includes thorough searching on all the trays and shelves for crumbs and sugar strands, after Rosie has cleaned, to present at the magnificent feast.

This fabulous banquet, that awaits The Blinks at the end of the get together, allows The Blinks to fuel up for the next day and celebrates hard work.

Stage 2...***A good start.*** This part comprises of The Blinks who are involved with a child and everything is going well. These Blinks use the time to learn from each other's tales of the day and start thinking what they can do next. This stage is also important for topping up their feel good bucket, which is then shared with children during the project.

All of Stage 2 happens on the vanilla

slice board, in the main display cabinet, furthest corner from the bakery's entrance. This tends to be the least busy stage of Blinkery. Because most Blinks' involvement presents lots of hurdles and issues, they tend to be in Stage 3. Just like you and me, no Blinks' work is easy, but when things are difficult, rather than stop trying, they try harder.

Stage 3...***Help!*** This being the busiest meeting point, needs the biggest area, and so happens on the wooden bread shelves that cover the whole back wall of the bakery, behind the display counter. This stage is usually known as Blink School!

Lots of discussions, learning, and more importantly listening to the Wise Ones, helps the Blinks keep improving and able to do their job the best they can. The Blinks understand the importance of listening, because only then might they pick up new gems of information that could make tomorrow a better day.

Stage 4...***Eye spy.*** The Blinks that have finished a project, and the young person they have helped has worked hard to improve their situation, are part of this penultimate stage. This stage happens on the fairy cake trays, in the window of the bakery. This phase is the most private of the stages, as it happens under large white sheets of kitchen paper, making The Blinks feel like they are hiding somewhere fun!

This is one of the nicest stages of The Blink cycle, as all Blinks hope that the child in question has made huge progress and has lots of tips in order to feel stronger in the future. The Blinks, however, do not move on to another project until they are 100% sure that all is right.

This means that the real feelings of success only begin after the observation phase has occurred. The Blinks think of this as a watchful eye, should they need to be on hand to help if things slip slightly.

The Blinks also have two rules at this stage;

1. Each child must tell at least one person, who they trust, about how they have been feeling recently and how they are feeling now. The Blinks see this as a very important part of their work for many reasons.

   All children need to know that they have someone who they can trust, whether it is a friend, teacher or family member. (Also, by sharing ourselves with other people, we ask them to be part of our lives so they can look after and care for us when we need it most.)

   This rule also allows The Blinks to feel that they can move on to the next stage with peace of mind. By knowing that each child is safe and cared for, with a level support in place, the circle of Blink magic is complete.

2. Children must never mention The Blinks help. Those who have done in the past very quickly wished that they had not! The Blinks' input stops from the very moment that those words are uttered; and Blink magic, if looked after, can live long in the hearts of grateful children.

Stage 5... ***Whey hey!*** As soon as The Blinks have a sense of satisfaction that each child has found their life to be in a better place, then a celebration of good work can begin. For seven whole days after the project ends, beginning at midnight the following day, a period of wonderfulness begins.

This time allows The Blinks to restock each positive value in their souls. This is essential to continue The Blinks success, especially after donating their hearts to whoever has just needed their help. Blinks do whatever they feel will make the seven days as fabulous as can be.

Older, wiser Blinks rest, eat the finest of sugar dough and share a sense of contentment. Younger Blinks embrace their feelings of a job well done and revel in whatever delights brings them deep joy.

All Blinks understand the system inside out (stories of the older Blinks suggest that fluff ball number 98 has something to do with The Blinks knowing the system) and so head to where they should be when Chief Blinks gives the sign.

However, before The Blinks are sent on their way, to whichever stage they are in, each meeting starts with a short get together and tonight for some reason The Blinks were more lively than normal.

Chapter 4

Choices

Robbie stood looking at his front door for ages. His brain was flooded with things that he could do, but he had no idea which was going to be the best one.

- Should he knock on the door and then Mum will know something has happened?
- Should he run back to school as soon as possible before anyone realised he had gone?
- Should he climb over the locked gate and hide in the bottom of the garden for the rest of the day?

This is when Robbie always struggled.

His brain was pretty good with coming up with choices, that was not the problem; it was knowing which choice was the best choice, that Robbie found difficult.

Robbie usually put his head in the sand, trying to ignore what seemed like too difficult a decision. Sometimes though, Robbie went with whatever choice was in his head at that time and did it without thinking. It was these quick reactions that tended to get him in the most trouble.

Robbie was still staring at the door, not knowing what to do at all, when he heard his neighbour Mr Benson unlocking his front door. Robbie's brain was flooded again with choices that he had no idea what to do with. One thought, that seemed to stick around longer than the others, was that he should quickly hide underneath the bush that separated the two gardens.

As Robbie dived head first into the thick

privet, his body jerked away from the sharp branches and hard ground which his knees fell upon, and then he came face to face with Archie, Mr Benson's cat! Who was more surprised at this point we will never know, but Archie thought of one choice and one choice only and that was...

"MMMMEEEOOOOWWWWW!" Archie kicked up dust and dead leaves as he escaped his once relaxing hideaway.

"Archie, what on earth's the matter? Come here pusssss, pusssss, pusss," said Mr Benson, who was staring curiously at the hedge, rather than at a very startled Archie.

Robbie hoped that if he kept still he would not be noticed, and could stay there, and hide away from what had happened today. However, keeping your eyes shut as tightly as possible with your head millimetres away from months of moulted cat fur and dried mud was a recipe for one almighty sneeze!

"Aaaatishooooo." Robbie sneezed, scratching his head further on the spikes of the hedge.

"Whoooooaaarrr," echoed Mr Benson. He had, just at that moment, thought that he had detected something strange in the thicket and so was within showering distance of the sneeze's force. "Is that you Robbie? What are you doing down there? Shouldn't you be at school?"

Robbie reversed himself out of the spikey greenery, stood up, ignoring Mr Benson, and headed towards his front door. At that moment, Robbie was scared, teary, sore from all the scratches, and the most alone he had ever felt. As he stood there looking at the letterbox, feeling lost and helpless, he heard the telephone ring from inside the house and the sound of Mum's feet coming down the stairs.

"Does your mum know you're not at school, Robbie?" repeated Mr Benson.

Although Mr Benson was trying to be

nice to Robbie at that moment, sadly, history between the neighbours hadn't always been good. Mr Tucker and Mr Benson had many disagreements over the years, and today that was all Robbie could think of.

Robbie bolted from his garden and started running with all his might to wherever his next safe haven might be. Behind him, his Mum, who he guessed was now fully aware of what had happened at school, was shouting at him to come back; whilst in between, having a set to with Mr Benson, wanting to know what he had done to her son to cause him to be so upset.

Robbie glanced over his shoulder to see Mr Benson shaking his head as he walked into his house. He knew Mr Benson would be thinking that all the Tuckers were the same!

Robbie knew he was heading for nowhere and if he didn't start making better choices soon, nowhere was where his life would end up! As he ran past Mums' taking toddlers to playgroup, elderly people strolling home with the morning paper, his eyes started burning from holding back the tears. He felt like the dam in his tear ducts was going to crumble any minute and once the floodgates opened, he might not be able to stop.

Tired and upset Robbie finally stumbled upon an area of unused garages and slid down the wall. The knot in his stomach had never felt so big; his breathing had never been so fast and his thoughts had never felt so sad.

Robbie jumped up in a flash and kicked a tin can ferociously at the garage door. The sound of metal on metal bellowed around the garage space, creating a raging melody. That had felt good, in fact, that had been the best he had felt all morning, so he did it again.

He finally let his volcano erupt and with a torrent of force it blew. Robbie even began shouting and grunting to try and rid his body of the feelings that were controlling him and his thoughts of being a failure.

Without realising it, Robbie was being watched by someone working in one of the garages a few doors up and who knew only too well what Robbie was feeling right now.

Cale felt like he was watching himself, when he was younger. He still knew that feeling of deep sadness that dominated your thoughts. This was why he was working on his own in a crumbling garage, on a car that could only be described as a 'huge heap of junk', rather than being at college with the friends he once had.

Cale was also flooded with choices. Even though he was many years older than Robbie, he still had the same issue of not feeling confident in what was the best thing to do. The main problem for Cale was that he had always been known on the estate as 'the bad lad'. Whoever this kid was, he would know of him and probably be scared of him, even if he did try to help. So Cale went back to his tinkering.

Robbie was starting to slow down,

feeling exhausted and no longer having the strength to kick anything anymore. Robbie's anger had left. What remained was fear and worry about how he was going to explain all of this, and the driest mouth he had ever had. As he strolled down past the garages, he noticed one had the front up, with music coming from inside.

Curiosity took Robbie closer and closer until he found himself peeping on an older lad tinkering with a rusty old banger of a car.

"Feeling better now?" asked Cale, not even lifting his head from the job that he wasn't doing very well.

"Erm... sorry, I didn't know anyone was here. I thought all these garages were being knocked down because no one used them," said Robbie. He was feeling a bit nervous as he was sure that this was one of the lads on the estate that was known to be nothing but trouble.

"Can you pass me that spanner, off the side there? The one with the red tape around the handle," asked Cale.

Robbie sheepishly walked behind the lad and scanned the dirty shelf that was covered in tools, and empty cans of pop. He felt relieved when he saw the tool with red tape on it, because he wasn't really sure what a spanner was and he didn't want to get on the wrong side of this lad.

"Here you are," whispered Robbie. He wondered whether he should get out of there as quickly as possible, but the lad's actions didn't feel threatening.

"Get yourself a can of coke out of that carrier bag, if you want. Thirsty work being that angry," mumbled Cale, still not raising his head from the imaginary bolt he was trying to tighten.

"Err, no. I'm ok thanks. I should go really," replied Robbie, hoping not to sound too nervous or weak.

"Alright, whatever you want. I'm Cale by the way." Cale then pulled his head out from under the car bonnet and nodded to Robbie, in a way that made Robbie feel understood. "I'm here most days, doing nothing more than this with my rubbish life. So if you ever want to compare rubbish lives, you know where I am and I bet I'd win." Cale winked with a half-smile.

"I'm Robbie, and today has been the worst day of my life. I'm in big big trouble and I don't know what to do to get myself out of it," said Robbie, feeling ashamed.

"I had many days like you, Robbie, hundreds; in fact nearly every day for me as a kid was like that, so you don't need to tell me about what you are feeling. I was the angry champion. I even got kicked out of school for it. They wouldn't have me back, so you don't need to feel ashamed in front of me. I'm the one who is ashamed, as I haven't changed." Cale lowered his head. 'I don't know how a young boy like you has made me start talking so honestly about his my life. But it's a good thing.'

Robbie and Cale chatted away about life for longer than Robbie ever intended. He found he was fascinated by how this person, who the estate feared, could actually be so sound.

Someone else had been observing the series of events that morning too. She felt like her tiny brain was going to burst with what she had collected in such a short space of time. Surely Robbie was the perfect project, and she felt confident that this had all the ingredients for the magic to occur.

Chapter 5

Who will win?

Blink 1970 – Chika Change- Your-Thoughts knew that it would seem a long wait until she could put forward Robbie's case at the midnight meeting tonight. What could she do to make sure that the time was used wisely?

Chika Change-Your-Thoughts tiptoed across the rooftops of the garages, leaving the chatting of Robbie and Cale behind her. She found herself thinking about the other children who she had been observing and who could also do with some Blink intervention. She reminded herself about some of the children who had not been ready in the past and whether one or two of them might need a second visit just to check if the time was right now.

Her first stop was Christian.

Christian – age 12, was one of the older children that Chika Change-Your-Thoughts was observing and had not long been in Secondary school. He was finding Y7 difficult because he didn't like all the changes. Christian had loved his time at Croft House Primary School but was feeling that this bigger school felt a bit too grown up for him. He wasn't very good at being organised either and had already, six weeks in, notched up two detentions!

As Chika Change-Your-Thoughts arrived at Goldendale Secondary School, she could see Christian scrambling frantically in his rucksack for his planner. PE kit was scattered on the floor, exercise books were being dumped in piles by Christian's feet and an opened pencil case was accidently tipped out and the contents danced across the shiny corridor floor. Christian slumped onto the mound of chaos that lay in front of him.

Just as Christian was trying to understand what he was actually feeling at that moment, Mrs Ronan, his Head of Year, bent down beside him.

"Hi, Christian. Is everything okay?" asked Mrs Ronan warmly.

"Oh, err, yes, errm, no not really," mumbled Christian and a tiny tear popped out of the side of his eye.

"Come on, Christian. Come with me. Let's see if we can sort this for you. It looks like you need a moment to get yourself together," reassured Mrs Ronan, helping Christian scoop up his belongings.

Chika Change-Your-Thoughts knew that Christian was going to be alright. She recognised that what Christian was feeling was what every child, who had come to Goldendale over the last fifty years, had felt at some point. Chika Change-Your-Thoughts knew that when things are difficult, it is then that we all need to try just a little bit harder.

With Mrs Ronan's help, Chika Change-Your-Thoughts knew that Christian was going to get the information and support he needed to overcome this new stage in his life. This was not a thing that Chika Change-Your-Thoughts could save him from, as it was part of learning about life and more importantly the next stage of growing up.

As Chika Change-Your-Thoughts left Christian in the safe, caring hands of Mrs Ronan, she removed a tiny pad and pencil from her skirt lining and crossed Christian off her list with a satisfied smile. Now to see how Louise was doing.

Louise aged 8, was not at school today. She had refused to go because she was being bullied. Unfortunately, Louise's Grandma didn't always help Louise by only listening to her side of the story, and so seeing Louise as the victim. However, Louise's story was a difficult one and although Chika Change-Your-Thoughts had been observing her for a while, Louise sadly was not ready to make changes for the better.

Louise lived with her Grandma, because both her parents had re-married and Louise had not liked either new step-parent at *ALL*! Although she had lived at each new house, with her new bedroom and new step-siblings, Louise hated it all too much to move forward. She blamed everyone else for everything in her life that was wrong, and this kept her in an angry state most of the time.

Chika Change-Your-Thoughts suddenly realised the similarities between Louise and Robbie and how both of them were struggling with strong feelings of anger. There was, however, one big difference – honesty!

Louise was not being honest about her angry thoughts. She could not see any of it being due to anything that she did. She never recognised that what she did sometimes caused people and situations to react negatively. Many times Louise had thoughts in her head which somehow always made it someone else's fault, or that somehow what they had done had made her do it! Things like this:

1. Louise was asked by her teacher if she had brought her homework sheet back. This is how Louise responded...

   "You never gave me a homework sheet or told me to bring it back, so it's your fault that I haven't done it."

2. Grandma had commented that her bedroom was getting quite messy. Louise replied...

   "But I never have time because I always have to do

my homework and stuff."

3. When Louise was spoken to by a lunchtime supervisor for spoiling a game that some of the girls in her class had been playing. Louise said...

   "Well they deserved it because they told on me last week for hiding someone's bag, they are bullying me!"

This was why Chika Change-Your-Thoughts knew that Robbie was slightly more ready than Louise. Robbie knew only too well the role he played in what he did, and it made him feel worse every day. Robbie's actions made him sad because he was honest enough to look inside his head think about what he'd done.

Chika Change-Your-Thoughts removed the pad and pencil from her skirt for the second time and circled Louise's name.

She then put a big star next to it. This meant that Chika Change-Your-Thoughts would continue to keep a watchful eye on Louise in the hope that she could become ready for some Blink magic.

The next thing that needed to be done was for Chika Change-Your-Thoughts to remind herself of all the reasons why Robbie deserved her time and wisdom. It was always a tough call at the midnight meeting as to who would be picked at that time. Every Blink's sole desire was to help children improve their difficult situations and so they were at their happiest when a project was given the green light.

Chika Change-Your-Thoughts had not had a case that felt so worthy, or that made her feel so excited to get started for a while. Robbie had definitely won his place from all the children on her list, but could she convince The Executive Blinks Panel? She would have to wait until later to find out.

Chapter 6

999

Back at Robbie's house things were anything but exciting. In fact, quite a whirlwind of negative emotions was brewing. Mrs Tucker was beside herself with worry now. All she kept saying was "Where can he be?" or "How could you let this happen?" to various members of the school, who had come to look for and hopefully find Robbie.

Mr Benson stood in his garden looking on, not sure whether to try and help or not. He had been on the receiving end of Mr and Mrs Tuckers' short fuse more than once before, and today felt like it had enough elements to be one of those days. Though he did feel part of this, having been the last person to see Robbie, and had seen how distressed he had looked.

Mr Jones, the Headteacher of Croft House Primary School, approached Mrs Tucker after making his sixth phone call to the school to see if Robbie had returned.

"We have been looking for Robbie for 1 hour and 24 minutes now Mrs Tucker, is there anywhere else you think that he might have gone?" asked Mr Jones.

"I don't flipping know," replied Mrs Tucker, holding her head in her hands at this whole messy situation. She really didn't need this today. The last forty-eight hours had been the worst that she could remember for a while. That then made her think about the last worst day that had happened just over six years ago, and today being Mr Tuckers birthday as well, she suddenly burst into tears.

Mr Jones approached Mrs Tucker and gently clasped her hand, "Mrs Tucker, I'm sure that everything will be fine. Robbie is an intelligent boy who is clued up enough not to do anything silly. However, I do think that it might be best informing the police to get more help in bringing him home safely and quickly. Do you agree?"

A loud snort erupted from Mrs Tucker and as her head dropped a whimpering "yheehesss" gave Mr Jones the answer he needed. He knew what had to be done.

At the garages, Robbie and Cale were still chatting away and drinking pop, totally unaware of the time or the drama that was occurring at Robbie's house. Robbie had spent the last hour wondering how people could have got Cale so wrong. He seemed to be one of the nicest people he had met in a while, though some of Cale's stories did make Robbie feel that maybe his life wasn't as bad as he sometimes thought it was.

Cale also thought the same about Robbie. Many times, over the last hour, he had pondered as to why this poor kid was being left to feel so sad and lonely. How come no-one seemed to get him, but then he knew that feeling only too well. Cale, for the first time in his entire life, felt like he was doing something right. He was being responsible and it actually felt quite good.

Then Cale's maturity took another twist.

"Listen Robbie, I've had a lovely time chatting with you here. Do you know what? I think you are an ace kid, but listen, no ten-year-old can be out of school for this long without people getting bothered. I think you should be getting back mate, don't you?"

"I don't want to. I'm in so much trouble. Everyone's going to be mad at me and I'm scared," replied Robbie, biting his nails.

"I'm doing something with you today, Robbie, which I've never done in my whole life. This is all a bit weird for me if I'm honest. Normally I'd be the first person to tell you how to do it as wrong as possible. To just keep running and hiding, but eventually all the choices you make will get you labelled. My label is *'a waste of space'* and it is well and truly stuck, look!" Cale pretended to remove an imaginary sticker from his forehead which ended up making them both burst out laughing.

"Your label can be loads better Robbie, do you see?" continued Cale.

"Yes, I think I do," said Robbie. "Nobody's talked to me like this, ever. You make me feel more grown up, not like the naughty boy most people think I am. I'm going to do what's right. I better go and face it all and hopefully they will listen and understand like you did. Thank you, Cale. Can I come and see you again?"

"Ooh, I don't know about that. What would everybody think? I have a *'waste of space'* reputation to keep up, which has taken me years to build. I wouldn't want it all changing just cos you suddenly think I'm alright." Cale answered with a wink. This kid seemed to see him differently to how everyone else ever had.

"Alright then Cale, see you later. But only after school hours or on a weekend from now on, I promise," said Robbie. He started heading back towards whatever would be waiting for him at home and school.

"See you, kid. You'll be alright, cos you're the alright kind," said Cale. He was still in shock that he had just learned more about himself from a ten-year-old boy than he had in all his life years.

Just as Robbie turned the corner by the last garage, he noticed a police car parked up and several Police Officers talking to residents. As he carried on walking, he wondered what must have happened. He then thought about Cale and the stories of mischief that he had been up to recently, and hoped it wasn't Cale who was in trouble. As he passed several of the houses, he decided that he needed to let Cale know that something was going on before he went back and faced his own mess.

Robbie turned around and walked briskly to the garage space. However, unbeknown to him, he had been spotted by one of the police officers who were out looking for him, and who was now following him to see where he was going.

Robbie scuttled past the empty tin cans that he had not so long ago been taking all his anger out on. He rushed to the open garage door where Cale was still tinkering with probably the same nut!

"There are loads of police out on the road, Cale. I thought I'd better tell you in case they're looking for you," said Robbie.

"No, they won't be looking for me mate. I've been up to mischief too long. I'm too good to be caught. Thanks for looking out for me, though. Now go on, off you go, stop putting it off," ordered Cale gently pushing Robbie in the right direction.

Just then, a police car pulled up in front of Cale's garage and the female Police Officer, who had followed Robbie, and another male Police Officer got out.

"Robbie, it's ok you're not in trouble. We've been looking for you, because the school and your Mum are worried. We're going to get you home now, safe and sound. Get yourself in the back of the police car while I radio the others to say you are okay," said Paddy the Police Officer, removing the radio from his belt.

"So, Cale," said Florrie the other Police Officer, "Is this what you've lowered yourself to now. Hanging around with and hurting little kids who should be at school?"

"Oh, here we go. Yeah, whatever. Have you got nothing better to do than hang around some skanky old garages having a go at me?" replied Cale aggressively.

Suddenly another police car skidded in from the other entrance and halted in front of the car that Robbie was sat in. Two more Police Officers got out and started talking firmly with Cale.

"It's alright, Robbie. We won't let him hurt you again. He's a bad un that one. He's been in trouble all of his life. It all started going wrong when he was your age. We've wanted to get him for a while, but he's good, never leaves a trace. Well, he's slipped up today. This is very serious, assault and possible abduction," explained PC Paddy.

Robbie started crying. He felt he should say something then, but the events of the day had finally caught up on him and all he could do was sob.

As Florrie got in next to Robbie, the car engine started and they drove past Cale; who was now being forced into the back of the other police car.

Robbie felt sick. What had he done? He now felt even lonelier and was left with a similar situation that he always felt he was in - what should he do now? Would anyone believe him anyway, if he explained that Cale had actually helped him this morning? Today was going from bad to worse.

Chapter 7

More questions than answers

As the police car pulled up in front of Robbie's house, Robbie felt so many emotions, many of which he could not name. A few of the stronger feelings were obvious and familiar like;

- Fear – a mixture of being worried about what people were going to say and afraid that something bad is going to happen because of what he had done that morning.

- Nervousness – anxious of what the outcome of events is going to be.

- Sadness – this low mood and feeling

of distress made Robbie want to cry. Regularly. The sadder he got at the things that he had done, the more of a failure he felt and the quicker he got angry.

What Robbie didn't realise was that within his solar plexus (his feelings pot), sat there just above his tummy, were many other emotions too;

- Disgust – Robbie felt disgusted at himself for all the things he felt, did and was.

- Shame – this feeling made Robbie feel like he wanted to run away and never come back. It made him feel like everyone knew all the bad things about him and they could see all that was wrong with him.

- Loneliness – Robbie felt that most people didn't understood him, well apart from Amanda & Cale, but why would they like him now anyway? He felt no-one cared for him, he was an outsider, different from everyone else.

One thing Robbie did know was that he felt little, weak and sick and going into his house in the next few minutes was going to be one of the hardest things he had done, since that dreadful day when he saw his dad's coffin.

"Come on son, let's get you in," said PC Paddy. "They are all desperate to see you. You gave everyone a bit of a shock today."

Robbie gulped and rubbed his heavy head. "Am I in trouble?" Robbie asked.

"I think everyone will be pleased to see you, Robbie, so the talking might wait a while. They're going to want to know why this happened, but hopefully you can do that when you are ready," reassured the Police Officer, unlocking his seat belt and opening his car door.

Robbie's door opened and suddenly he felt vulnerable and exposed.

Together the two Police Officers and

Robbie walked down the path to his front door. Just as PC Florrie raised her hand to knock, the door was opened by Mr Jones.

"Hello, Robbie. Come on in. We've all been worried about you. Are you okay?" he said.

Robbie gave a half smile but knew the worst wasn't over yet.

Suddenly Mrs Tucker barged down the stairs. "What on earth have you been playing at today? Don't you think I have enough to deal with? I don't need this. You are grounded for a month and no computer screens for a week; do you hear me?" bellowed Mum.

What Robbie really wanted was a hug and to feel cared for, but Mum was too angry and this response triggered his anger again.

"I hate you, I hate everything," raged Robbie. He barged through the crowded hallway and ran upstairs to the safety of his bedroom. As he slammed the door, tears sprang from his eyes again and he slumped down the door and sobbed into his hands.

Downstairs he could hear muffled voices discussing the morning events, and what should happen next. Mrs Tucker was being calmed down by PC Florrie. Mr Jones was on his mobile phone to school, letting them know that Robbie was home. PC Paddy, was on his radio to the station finding out the latest about Cale.

After what seemed like hours to Robbie, but was actually fifteen minutes, there was a gentle knock on his door.

"Robbie, it's me, Mrs Medway, from school. It's going to be ok Robbie, you aren't in trouble. We know that you're not feeling happy at the moment. We also understand that things have been difficult for you and your family over the last few months. Could you open the door, Robbie, and let me know that you're alright?" asked Mrs Medway.

As Robbie stood up, he could see his t-shirt was stained with tears. He opened the door and stood with his shoulders sagging.

"Oh Robbie, you look exhausted. Do you feel ready to come downstairs? Hopefully we can think about going back to school, if you feel up to it?" Mrs Medway suggested calmly.

"I don't want to. My Mum is going to have another go at me, then Mr Jones and...." Robbie burst into tears again.

"Hey, hey. Nobody is going to have a go at you. Your Mum has been crying too. She feels dreadful at what she said, Robbie. Sometimes grown-ups have feelings they struggle to cope with too you know. Today is a very difficult day for your Mum as well. She and your Dad had always planned to go to New York for their forty-fifth birthdays, so not only is she missing your Dad today, she is missing their dream," explained Mrs Medway.

"Come on let's get you two in each other's arms, where I think you both need to be at the moment. Do you think that you can do that, Robbie?"

Robbie so desperately needed a hug from Mum. Cuddles are gifts of love, his Mum always used to say and now felt like the right time to give and receive. He just hoped his Mum felt the same.

"Okay." Robbie nodded. He remembered Amanda once telling him that if you weren't sure what to do in a situation, do the kindest thing and now felt like one of those times.

As they walked down the stairs, Robbie could hear the sound of police radios crackling and Mrs Tucker blowing her nose coming from the dining room. From the living room came the gentle undertone of children's TV which was no doubt to entertain his sick brothers, who would be wrapped in duvets on the settee.

As Robbie opened the door, Mrs Tucker started crying again. Robbie hated seeing his Mum like this. In fact, the last time he had seen his Mum really crying was at the Funeral and this reminded him once again of that dreadful day. Robbie scurried over to her and wrapped his arms around her neck.

"I'm so sorry for shouting, Robbie. I've been really worried and seeing you made me feel relieved, but cross too. What is the matter darling? Why are you are so sad and angry all the time?" asked Mum.

Dilemma time again! Did Mum really want him to answer? Could he answer that question straight away? Did he even know the answer?

Robbie decided to just hug.

Do the kindest thing, he heard Amanda say in his head. So, because his feelings were still not great, he thought it best to keep his mouth shut and show kindness instead.

"We are going to go now, Mrs Tucker," explained PC Florrie. "We need to head down to the station and get some answers from a young person who was taken into custody earlier. If you need us at all, please don't hesitate to contact us."

"Thank you both for all your help

finding Robbie. I really do appreciate it." said Mum to PC Florrie, who had been a calming influence when Mrs Tucker desperately needed it.

"Yes, I think it might be better if we get back to school too, Mrs Tucker," echoed Mr Jones. "Robbie we would love you to join us. You're not in trouble, I promise. We would like to spend some time with you though, to see how we can make all this better for you. Are you okay with that?"

"Yes. I want to go back to school Mum. Is that all right?" asked Robbie.

"Of course, son. Whatever you feel is best for you. We can talk about it later, and I promise not to get cross." Mum smiled, with a hint of embarrassment.

"Right then, Robbie. If we get a move on we should be back just in time for lunch," said Mrs Medway. "We will look after him, Mrs Tucker. I promise you he is in good hands. I will give you a ring later to discuss what we're going to do to move this forward for all of you."

Mrs Tucker stood at the front door thanking them all for their time and support. She shook hands with Mr Jones and Mrs Medway and pulled Robbie in for one last hug and kiss.

With that Robbie and Mrs Medway got into Mr Jones's car and began part two of the school day. Robbie felt relieved that he was going to finally get some help. However, he couldn't stop thinking about Cale and who was supporting him.

Chapter 8

Shelf fright!

Chika Change-Your-Thoughts notepad was bulging with things that justified why she needed to champion Robbie's story. In fact there was so much potential work to do Chika Change-Your-Thoughts might need to call on the help of some Blinks friends along the way.

As Sheffoold approached darkness, all the lamp posts began illuminating into action. The Blinks who had scattered themselves across the City started tip-toeing towards Rosie's Bakery ready for the wonders of the midnightly meeting.

Peter Practise intended to get there early as he had felt almost naked throughout the day without the red button at the end of his hat! He had to find it before the other Blinks arrived, as finding something in a crowd is never easy.

Blink 1415 Imogen I–Can-Do-It was looking forward to the start of her seven days of fun, as she had finished a very rewarding project with a girl called Clare aged 7. This project had taken many months and not been easy. Clare, you see had become a really, really fussy eater. In fact, Clare had actually become an almost not-eater!

Her parents had tried everything from gentle probing to punishment if she refused to eat, to ignoring, to as a last, resort getting cross. However nothing persuaded Clare to try anything new, or old if she didn't want to.

The more people tried to get Clare to eat, the more stressed and angry about it she became and this hugely affected her appetite. The issue wasn't about her eating new things it was about the distressing feelings that were around at meal times and nearly always directed at her.

Imogen I-Can-Do-It had recognised this as being quite a common problem and so was able to guide it with confidence in the right direction. This project involved more working with parents and the other adults in her life than it was working with Clare.

It was six little words that started to make all the difference. Yes, six little words. What do you think that they might be?

a) "Eat it or you are grounded."

b) "Eat it or you won't grow."

c) "No pudding unless you eat mains."

d) "It is rude to not eat."

e) "You don't have to eat it."

So which phrase do you think took away all of the stress around food for Clare? The answer is...e!

Imogen I-Can-Do-It spent lots of time in adults inner ears explaining how Clare's eating was not about the food, it was about the pressure that she was having put on her. By removing the distress and telling Clare that she did not have to eat it, Clare became curious. The pressure was off and curiosity moved in!

Clare was now a much better eater and her parents had become much happier parents. Also, Imogen I-Can-Do-It was to be rewarded with seven days of fun and frolics to celebrate all her hard work and efforts, whoop!

Chika Change-Your-Thoughts was also ready; as ready as she had ever been. She had spent most of the afternoon and evening planning what to say and how best to present Robbie's plight. She also wanted to get to the bakery early to get a good spot near the front.

As Chika Change-Your-Thoughts arrived, she found Peter Practise trawling the trays on the bakery window. He was steadily pacing out each centimetre while scanning from left to right in the hope of finding his beloved button.

What Peter Practise had learned from this was that he did not realise how much he loved that little red button until he had lost it. Maybe if he had looked after it better he wouldn't have lost it. He would most definitely appreciate it more than ever when he got it back.

Chika Change-Your-Thoughts went over and stood next to him. "Can I help you in anyway Peter Practise, have you lost something?"

"Hi Chika Change-Your-Thoughts, oh that would be great. I lost the little red button off my hat last night and I've felt so sad without it. I'm hoping to find it before the meeting gets underway."

"Right then, four eyes are better than two. You carry on with these trays and I will do the cabinet by the till," said Chika Change-Your-Thoughts.

"Thank you. We only have ten minutes before everyone will start arriving," said Peter Practise.

Sadly neither Peter Practise nor Chika Change-Your-Thoughts found the button before the meeting began, as it was still sat safely inside the pocket of Rosie's white baking jacket. Nevertheless, Chika Change-Your-Thoughts promised Peter Practise that they would not give up and would stay behind at the end if time allowed.

"Sssshhhhhhhhhh. Order, order," commanded Chief Blink. She took her place on the platform from which she spoke most evenings. "I do hope this evening finds you all well and thank you once again for all your hard work and effort in helping the children of Sheffoold."

A ripple of warmth escaped from the hearts of The Blinks and caused them to burst into a cheer.

"Okay, Blinks, you all know the stage that you are in and the places that you should be. We will reunite for the feast in ninety minutes. Enjoy," said Chief Blink.

With that, a chaotic scattering erupted.

Chika Change-Your-Thoughts had perched herself as close to the chocolate éclair tray as possible so that she did not waste any time. As the other Blinks arrived, many of them went straight on to prepare the sugar dough buffet, as they had no children to put forward.

Chika Change-Your-Thoughts hoped that tonight it might be just her and she could spend the time with one of the Wise Ones. Just then two other Blinks arrived to put forward their cases.

All the Blinks knew that this was

the time to champion the children of Sheffoold, who were having a difficult time. But the need had to be the right need.

Blink 30321 – Terry Try-Your-Best was a well-respected Wise One, who had entertained The Blinks for many, many years with tales and stories of past projects. Tonight, it was his job to hear The Blinks cases and see who got the green light to move to stage 2 tomorrow.

"Good evening Miranda Make-It-Happen, Chika Change-Your-Thoughts, and Lottie Love-Life," said Terry Try-Your-Best. "So, you have all found potential children to work with and now feel that each case is ready for some work to begin."

There was a chorus of agreement, with nodding heads and enthusiastic smiles.

"Miranda Make-It-Happen, please could you begin," asked Terry Try-Your-Best.

"Of course," said Miranda Make-It-

Happen. "My child is a boy called Alex, aged 8, whose new puppy has sadly just died from Parvovirus; a horrible illness that affects dogs. He is distraught and has been crying now for days. I am hoping to help him through this difficult time."

"Thank you, Miranda Make-It-Happen. Understandably, it's a difficult time for Alex. Let us now hear the next case. Chika Change-Your-Thoughts tell us about your child," said Terry Try-Your-Best.

Chika Change-Your-Thoughts climbed to the shelf at the top of the tray and, with her notepad in hand, was ready to explain all about Robbie. Suddenly Chika Change-Your-Thoughts brain was flooded with how important this was and how much she cared about this case and her mouth failed to open. Nothing came out, not even a squeak.

"Would you like a drink of water, Chika Change-Your-Thoughts?" asked Terry Try-Your-Best.

Still nothing was uttered from Chika Change-Your-Thoughts.

"Let's do this in a different order," said Terry Try-Your-Best. "Lottie Love-Life, who is your project about?"

"Hi, everyone. My project involves David, who is 11 and keeps getting detentions because he is so disorganised. He desperately needs some help to try and get a system in place. Also his parents are starting to lose patience with him too and this is making the situation worse," explained Lottie Love-Life.

"Thank you, Lottie Love-Life. Yes, another problem that is causing distress for David and his family. So, Chika Change-Your-Thoughts, are you ready to tell us about your young person now?"

Just then Peter Practise, who was supposed to be preparing the sugar dough buffet, but was instead still hunting for his beloved button, asked if he could have a quick word with Chika Change-Your-

Thoughts.

"Yes, of course Peter Practise. If you think it might help," answered Terry Try-Your-Best.

"This means a lot to you, doesn't it Chika Change-Your-Thoughts?" began Peter Practise. "You obviously care a lot about this person and their story, but it is causing your brain to become hi-jacked. Sometimes when we really want something a lot, it can affect our abilities. Look at your notepad. You have been reading and re-reading it the whole time you have been here. You don't need the pad. What you want to say is in your heart. You can do this, I know you can."

Chika Change-Your-Thoughts knew that Peter Practise was right. She did care so much and it was affecting her ability to do this for Robbie. She took a deep breath, activated her calm brain and launched into all the evidence that she had gathered about Robbie, his family circumstances and even Cale.

Peter Practise was right. She didn't need the pad at all; Robbie's issues were flowing through every vein in her body. She just hoped that her belief and passion for this case impressed Terry Try-Your-Best.

A tiny applause began. Both Miranda Make-It-Happen and Lottie Live-life knew how hard that had been for Chika Change-Your-Thoughts, and also knew how important this case was to her. This thought was also mirrored by Terry Try-Your-Best.

Everyone agreed that Robbie was most needy of The Blinks intervention. Terry Try-Your-Best explained that although Alex was having a difficult time, sometimes time is the healer and losing something that we love hurts. No Blink can make that situation better.

And David, well, maybe he just needed to get it wrong enough times until his reflective brain kicked in and provided some solutions. Making mistakes is a major part of the learning process, because if we don't make mistakes we are not learning. David was learning and eventually he would get the lesson and feel proud.

Robbie was most definitely the most worthy of The Blinks help as this involved showing him and his family how to do things differently and that needed action and understanding. Chika Change-Your-Thoughts was delighted and could not wait to help move things on for Robbie. However, she also promised to support her new special friend, Peter Practise, to find his red button, because one good favour deserves another, so that is what she would do!

Chapter 9

Swimming against the tide

Back at school Robbie was feeling calmer, but exhausted. The events of the morning had certainly taken their toll on him, and what he really needed was to see Amanda. He knew that morning lessons would be finishing soon and he could get back to feeling normal.

Mr Jones had let Robbie sit in the ICT suite with Mrs Lomas, so that he wasn't alone. There was no pressure to talk; in fact, they were currently having some fun playing a game that Mrs Lomas found to be a good distraction in times of need.

As the bell rang for lunch, Robbie broached the subject of going out to play with his friends.

"Of course, Robbie. No problem at all. However, will you promise me that if you need anything or are feeling upset or angry, you will come and find me straight away? I will be in the office or the staff room all lunch time. Deal?" asked Mrs Lomas, holding out her hand to seal the agreement.

"Deal." Robbie smiled, offering his hand for a firm handshake of approval.

With that, Robbie wandered over to the cloakroom outside his classroom hoping that Amanda would soon arrive there. As he was waiting for the classes to empty, he noticed the glances and glares from the kids in his year group. He knew only too well that word soon got around the playground and his running out of school was bound to be major news.

After what seemed like far too long,

Amanda came out.

"Hey, Robbie, are you okay? I have been worried about you," whispered Amanda with a warm smile.

"I am now, that I'm with you. To be honest, today has been pretty rubbish. Is everyone talking about what I did to Ben?" asked Robbie, dreading the answer.

"Yeah, a bit. But only because it was the most exciting thing that has happened here for a while," laughed Amanda, trying not to cause Robbie any more distress. "How about we go and sit up on the field until we get called in for lunch?"

"Great plan," said Robbie.

Amanda and Robbie chatted all lunchtime, with only the short pause for cottage pie, carrots and peas, followed by jam roly poly and custard. Nobody said anything to Robbie at all. Although everyone was desperate to know what had happened and why, they knew that only

Amanda had the honour to talk to Robbie about something like this.

The afternoon turned out to be quite enjoyable for Robbie. He had his two favourite subjects of science and art. In fact, at one point, Robbie felt pleased that he couldn't have picked a better day to have had a morning crisis! Just before the end of the session Mrs Lomas popped back to see Robbie and check on how he was feeling.

"I'm fine thanks, Mrs Lomas. This afternoon has been fun," said Robbie.

"How is that anger feeling?" asked Mrs Lomas. "Is it still around?"

"I always feel a bit angry, but at the moment I would say it isn't too bad."

"Right now, how many would you give your anger out of ten? If zero is the lowest it could be and ten is the highest it could be?" said Mrs Lomas.

"Erm...right now I think it would be a 4,"

said Robbie. "Though I was definitely at least a nine this morning."

"Well, I'm so glad that you're feeling calmer. Let's hope that tomorrow is even better. You know where I am if you ever need to talk or have some time out. Will you try and remember that for me, Robbie? Also is there anything that you might need to say to Ben?" said Mrs Lomas.

"Sorry. I will," said Robbie, half liking the fact that Mrs Lomas had taken the time to come and see him. However, the other half did not want to be reminded of what had happened earlier, especially now he was so close to going home. "Yes I will say sorry to Ben, I promise to do that as soon as I go back in to the classroom."

"Thank you Robbie, and well done for realising that. Ben needs to hear those words from you before he goes home," said Mrs Lomas.

Home turned out to be okay too. It was

still chaotic; with groggy Charlie and Lex and Vanessa still as moody as ever. Although, he did think that she seemed to be nicer to him, almost as if she understood more. Mum was pretty much the same which was fine by Robbie. He had walked home wondering if she was going to be more cross than she had been, and what she was going to say to him about the morning's events.

"Hi Robbie, stick that bin bag in the black bin will you, please. How was your afternoon, son?" asked Mum, as she greeted him at the kitchen door.

"Good thanks, Mum. Are you still cross with me?" muttered Robbie, nervously.

"No, it's all forgotten about. We all had a rubbish start to the day. If you're feeling ok, that is fine by me. I've made your Dad's favourite for tea to celebrate his birthday; Spanish Chicken and Rice. I thought we could sit round together and try and end the day better than it started," said Mum.

"Thanks, Mum. I'm just going to watch TV for a bit." Robbie dumped his school bag in the usual spot by the dining table.

Chika Change-Your-Thoughts watched from the top of one of the picture frames. There was so much work that she needed to do with Robbie and his Mum. The last thing that Robbie needed was for everything to be forgotten. What he really needed was time with his Mum to try and understand the deep feelings that he was having and how best to manage them.

The question was, could she get that conversation to happen before bedtime, as it needed to be done today for it to have the biggest and best impact. Chika Change-Your-Thoughts decided to risk a tricky manoeuvre and try to access Mum's inner thinking while she was awake.

How was she going to do it? The inner ear was a possibility as was the nostril, but suddenly Mrs Tucker gave Chika

Change-Your-Thoughts the perfect opportunity.

The events of the day, week, months and years had affected Mum more than she wanted to accept. The smell of the chicken, peppers, chorizo and tomatoes bubbling away on the oven top was the catalyst to Mum releasing a river of tears. Chika Change-Your-Thoughts was known to be a strong swimmer and so she felt confident enough to enter through the tear duct and swim upstream!

Reducing herself to the smallest size that The Blinks can make themselves, Chika Change-Your-Thoughts tiptoed underneath Mrs Tucker's hands and squeezed herself inwards. This was harder than she expected. The tears were coming out with great force. More than once Chika Change-Your-Thoughts nearly got washed out, especially when a nose blow occurred.

The inner workings of Mrs Tucker's mind were very cluttered. There were lots of boxes of sadness, a huge area of anger and many other emotions that Chika Change-Your-Thoughts realised needed sorting out, if Mum was to feel happier than she had been feeling over the last few years.

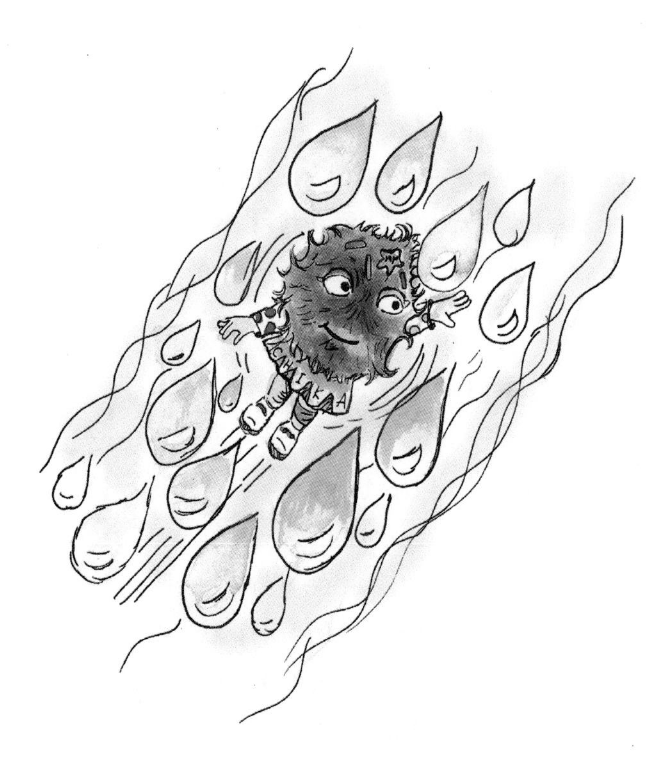

Eventually, a very dusty, derelict part of Mum's brain was found; the empathy section. Situated in the frontal lobe, just behind the forehead was the bit that Chika Change-Your-Thoughts needed to get to, to help Mum help Robbie.

With a few tweaks here, some wisdom sharing there and a scattering of information dust; the empathy section was already starting to pulsate with life thoughts again. One last thing that needed doing was to untangle some of the synapses (brain pathways) and reconnect other important sections.

As Chika Change-Your-Thoughts were busily working away, Mrs Tucker was being rebooted without even realising it. The only thing that made her think that things weren't quite right was that her facial expressions were changing very quickly from one emotion to another! As she noticed this happening, she started counting and recorded eight different looks in two minutes!

More importantly, Mrs Tucker began

to move her thoughts from the deep, sad parts of her brain, where she had been stuck for the last few years. Suddenly, she began to feel a deeper understanding of how unhappy Robbie must have been feeling earlier that day. The tears streamed again when she realised how cross she had been with him when he had returned home.

How could she have been so blind? How could she have been so thoughtless when her son needed her the most? Robbie had wanted her earlier and she had got angry at him for expressing feelings that he didn't know how to deal with.

Mrs Tucker knew these feelings only too well, but she was the adult. She needed to help Robbie to understand them, and more than that, to let him know that she was there for him.

Mum had a huge urge to spend some quality time with Robbie. She turned off the hobs, gave her eyes a quick wipe and headed towards the living room.

"Robbie. Robbie, where are you my darling? I think you and I need to have a little talk, so that we can make all this better together."

Chika Change-Your-Thoughts smiled from the inner workings of Mrs Tucker's mind. Next was to help Robbie learn that he was in control of his anger and not his anger in control of him!

Chapter 10

Out of your depth!

In the police cell, Cale was still waiting to be interviewed over the numerous accounts of mischief that the police could match to him. He was furious that on the one day in his whole life when he felt that he had actually done something good, he was in fact in more trouble than ever!

These thoughts were sending all kinds of negative messages to his anger zone which sat deep in his solar plexus. He found himself thinking;

- What is the point in being different, people will always think I am the same?

- I should have told that kid to carry on making the choices he was making. Kids like him and Robbie were always going to have a difficult time.
- The police are out to get me.
- No-one listens to me, or ever has.
- Who did you think you were earlier, trying to be someone better? You are a loser, always have been and always will be.

Suddenly, all the negative thoughts got too much. Cale jumped up from the hard bed and kicked the plastic bin next to the sink. His mind flashed back to watching Robbie outside the garages. He was seventeen and still behaving like a ten-year-old, who at that time was actually probably behaving like a six-year-old!

That made Cale feel even more cross, and he started shouting aggressively at the cell's guard.

Chika Change-Your-Thoughts was

hiding in the corner of the barred window frame. This was an unusual one for her as Cale wasn't officially a child and was not directly involved with Robbie like Mrs Tucker was, but boy did he need her help. More so, Chika Change-Your-Thoughts felt that with some Blink magic Cale could, in fact, become more of the person he was earlier that day and be a great help to Robbie and others.

Checking that her notepad was in place and that her skirt was straight, she decided that she would seize the moment.

"Hi, Cale. You seem very distressed at the moment, so I thought I would introduce myself. I am Chika Change-Your-Thoughts. Nice to meet you," she said, offering out her tiny hand for a possible handshake.

"Whoooaaa there," spluttered Cale. He became rooted to the spot with shock, but not fearful at all. "I'm seventeen and I don't believe in fairies. I'm not imagining this, am I? Whoooaaaa!"

"No, you are not imaging this at all. I must correct you though. I am not a fairy. I am in fact a Blink. Blink 1970 to be precise, and my job, along with all the other Blinks in Sheffoold and across the world, is to help children who are having a tough time in life," said Chika Change-Your-Thoughts.

"Eh? I'm no kid. I'm seventeen. Actually, in three weeks I'll be 18. What are you doing coming to me?" asked Cale, still resistant to Chika Change-Your-Thoughts.

"You met someone today who I have just started working with; a boy called Robbie. Part of the work I'm doing with him involves looking at all the best possible ways to make things better for him. If you don't mind me saying, you were brilliant earlier. I was very impressed. I'm here partly because I think you and I could work together to help him, but also a bit of Blink magic could massively help you too, if you will let me," said Chika Change-Your-Thoughts.

Cale was baffled by what was happening, but found himself striking up a conversation with Chika Change-Your-Thoughts regardless.

"Yeah, Robbie's a good kid. No point you or me helping him though, it's all over. Once you get a name for yourself that's it, nothing will change. Nice kid, but too late," said Cale. "And with regards to me, well, thanks for the offer. But like I just said, too little too late. My life's ruined and I just have to live with that, end of."

"Do you *really* believe that Cale? I mean really? Especially after today, weren't you impressed with yourself? I know I was. The only way things continue to stay the same is if you don't do anything different. Today, if I'm right, you did something different. And my guess is you quite liked it. I know Robbie did," said Chika Change-Your-Thoughts.

"Well, yeah, I suppose I did. But what good has it done me. I'm here in a police cell about to get charged for something, anything and I probably wouldn't be here if I hadn't met the kid, so what is the point?" Cale ranted.

"Okay, let's look at this situation. Just before I introduced myself, you were aggressive, abusive, shouting and kicking things around this cell. What message is that giving the officer on duty?" asked Chika Change-Your-Thoughts.

"Well, that I'm not happy in here and I want to get out," said Cale.

"Possibly, but it's more likely telling him that you have the character of someone who has no control over his actions, is rude and violent, and is likely to make wrong choices," said Chika Change-Your-Thoughts. "If you keep on doing this he won't listen to a word that comes out of your mouth, because you're communicating more than enough with your behaviour. You know what will happen then…."

Cale was taking this discussion very seriously. "Yeah, I do. I'll get done for the way I'm behaving, not because of what I have or haven't done. And it will make me even more angry, and then it goes on and on and on. That's how my whole life has gone, one huge angry mess of injustice."

"Okay, so what can you do differently this time?" asked Chika Change-Your-Thoughts, with a hope that Cale could come up with the needed wisdom at this very important time.

"I need to…I could… grrrr, I'm just too cross at the moment to even think about doing things differently," said Cale.

"Right then, listen to this Cale and listen carefully. Think about these things;

- Why are you here?
- What did you do wrong today?

- What did you do right today?
- Do you want today to be a disaster?
- Do you want today to be a better day that could be the start of the rest of your life?"

"The truth will come out about today, I'm sure of it. So you can either be a hero or you can do something worse. What do YOU want it to be?" asked Chika Change-Your-Thoughts.

"It won't work," said Cale.

"How do you know?" replied Chika Change-Your-Thoughts. "Are you a fortune teller now?"

"Lovely as you are, Chika Change-Your-Thoughts, and I still can't quite believe I am having such a grown up chat with a piece of purple and orange fluff, it is me, Cale that you are talking to and it will never change." Cale felt very sad.

"How do you know?" asked Chika Change-Your-Thoughts, again. "Why don't you just try and do something different, anything, and see. You have nothing to lose. Try it as an experiment. You might just be surprised."

"Well, when you put it like that, I suppose I could. It might be more interesting as police interviews are so boring. They always go on and on until I lose it and they have to put me back in here," said Cale.

"Right, so in order to reduce your anger;"

- Think about the person who you were earlier. What qualities did you have? How did they make you feel?

- Rather than thinking that the police are after you, remember that they are doing their job.

- Tell the truth. You were not a trouble causer today, you were a hero.

- Think positive. Show them the new, more mature, wiser you.

- Do for yourself what you suggested to Robbie. Be your own best friend when you need it most.

Just as Chika Change-Your-Thoughts and Cale were finishing this conversation, two loud, determined knocks on the door jolted them into the present moment.

"Cale, you've got five minutes before I'll be taking you down to be interviewed.

That's five minutes to think about what happened earlier today. Okay?" said the on-duty Police Officer.

"Right, Cale, this is over to you. Show them something different today. Remember Robbie is not going to tell them anything bad. Don't let your negative thinking, or expectations of what you *think* is going to happen, stop you from making the right choices. I believe in you. You can do this. Do for it you and do it to show Robbie that people can change," said Chika Change-Your-Thoughts. They did a 'high five' to confirm it.

As the lock unbolted, Chika Change-Your-Thoughts winked and disappeared. Could this next half hour really be a life changing event for Cale? Well, there was only one way for him to find out.

Chapter 11

Word medicine

Back at the Tucker household Mum and Robbie were having a very special moment together, one that had never happened before.

Normally after arguments, no-one ever talked about what had gone on, why it had occurred or more importantly what could be done differently next time. This meant that Robbie and his family had become stuck in the same aggressive routine for years which had, in the long term, made everyone feel worse; and no-one felt worse than Robbie.

Robbie had even thought to himself as he was walking home from school that night, that he felt cross at how Mum had shouted at him when he was brought home by the police. He knew, however, that talking to Mum about it was pointless and apologies never happened. So as usual he would store those angry feelings away until something else happened and then he would let them out again!

So no-one was more surprised than Robbie when Mum came into the living room, lifted his legs off the sofa and sat down next to him resting his legs across her lap.

"How are you feeling sweetheart?" asked Mum. "Today has been a pretty eventful day."

"Have you been crying, Mum?" asked Robbie, desperate for it to not be because of him.

"Only a little bit. But don't you be worrying about me, this is about you.

I'm so sorry that I shouted at you earlier today. Some days it just gets too much for me and I feel so sad, and that makes me angry with life. I don't control it very well, do I?" asked Mum nervously.

Inside Robbie's head, the 'CHOICES' word rang out loud and clear again. Was he supposed to answer that question? Could he be honest and say how it really made him feel? Should he just pretend it was all okay and make Mum feel better? Was he smart enough to be honest but still make Mum feel alright at the end of it?

Robbie gulped and decided to go for it. Although this time with Mum was rare, it felt special and he wanted to make the most of it.

"You just seem to be in a bad mood all the time, Mum. That makes me feel as if you don't like me anymore and that makes me sad. I do understand it's since we lost Dad, but I hate the thought of us all being miserable forever because he died," said Robbie, wondering if he had said too much.

The words went deep into Mum's thoughts. Did the kids really think that she did not like them anymore? Was she always in a bad mood? Robbie's honesty jolted her into reality and she knew she was going to work at changing this situation for all of them.

"You're right Robbie. I am in a bad mood a lot of the time, but that's going to change. I can't bear the thought of you thinking that I don't like you anymore, as it's not true at all. I love you, and need all of you more than you will ever realise. Being in a bad mood doesn't give me the chance to show love and affection and for that I'm really sorry. You do know now that I love you with all my heart, don't you Robbie?"

This felt the right time for Robbie to make Mum feel better. "Of course I do.

You're my Mum. And you do know that I love *you* with all of my heart, don't you Mum?"

Robbie and Mum both burst out laughing and dived into each other's arms for a huge cuddle. From that moment all their sadness disappeared. So did the feelings of loneliness and the sense of failure that both of them had felt so intensely over the last few years. Their hearts had reconnected and it felt amazing to both of them.

"Do you forgive me, Robbie, for being distant when you needed me over the last few years?" started Mum.

"Of course," replied Robbie nuzzling himself closer towards her.

"You have taught me a lot today, and I'm so very proud of you. Things are going to get better, I promise. It's time for some changes and no-one needs to change more than me. Right, who wants Spanish chicken?" Mum squeezed Robbie so tightly that she could feel his heart beating.

"Thanks Mum, for the chat today. I really liked it. I'm going to make an effort too. Can I ask you one more thing before you go?" said Robbie.

In Mum's head, her old ways suddenly sprang into action. She really needed to get on with tea as the triplets would be hungry any minute, and the rice would only sit there for so long before it was ruined! However the word 'CHOICES' suddenly popped into her head too. What was more important than this special time with Robbie? The triplets could wait five more minutes and so could the rice! "Of course Robbie, what is it, love?"

Robbie then told her all about meeting Cale at the garages that morning. Mum was initially quite distressed, as she knew only too well the stories of that good for nothing lad. However, as the story went on and the way that Robbie spoke about

Cale, she too started to think that maybe he wasn't as bad as people made him out to be.

"But the thing is, Mum. The police took him away because they thought he had kidnapped me. He could get into loads of trouble for nothing. What can we do to help him?" pleaded Robbie.

"Mmm this is a tough one son. Right, come on; let's put our heads together while I'm cooking tea. This needs a plan, because I know how important this is to you," she said.

Robbie and Mum pondered many choices while the tea was simmering away. In the end, contacting PC Florrie seemed to be the best option. Though it would have to wait until after all the hungry mouths had been fed.

Teatime ran much more smoothly than normal. Mum was making a conscious effort not to be in a bad mood, and this seemed to wash over everyone else's mood too. Vanessa was definitely grunting less, and Robbie was convinced that she cracked a smile at one of Beth's jokes. Even the triplets seemed calmer.

Mum noticed the same things. Everyone around the dining table felt more united. Could this all be because something had changed in her head? Did her negative mood really affect how she saw things and how the kids behaved around her? The biggest change though was in Robbie.

His face looked different. His heavy brow had lifted. His shoulders had straightened out. He wasn't reacting to everything with aggression. As Robbie looked her way, she gave him a wink and a smile which instantly made him feel that things were going to be better.

Mum decided to seize the moment. "Right, kids. The last few years, months, weeks and days have been tough, really tough, but I think we have all suffered enough. I'm sorry if I have been grumpy and horrible, it was because I felt only grumpy and horrible things.

"We are a family and we're going to move forward together. You need me and I need you. So before we wish your Dad a happy forty-fifth birthday, can we give him the best present ever and promise that we will make more of an effort to help and support each other?"

Everyone but Vanessa agreed.

"I know I've got things wrong, but this is about us all starting to do things right. You haven't had any pocket money for ages Vanessa, but if you agree to be a more active part of the family, then we can start that from now," added Mum.

"Do I still have to do chores?" asked Vanessa.

"Absolutely, but we can make a rota up so everyone knows what they are doing and when," said Mum.

"Can we do chores?" echoed Charlie, Lex

and Beth desperate to be old enough to do some grown up things, but too young to realise how quickly the novelty would wear off!

"We're all going to help each other and have little jobs that make us work together as a team. We are also going to discuss our feelings more, and the things that have happened in our day, so that negative feelings don't build up and become a problem," explained Mum. "Now, though, we need to have a moment for your Dad, after three. One, two, three...."

"Happy Birthday, Dad. We miss you, Dad. We love you, Dad," chorused the family.

"Charlie, Lex and Beth can you clear the table, please? Robbie and Vanessa can you load the dishwasher and wipe the table and kitchen surfaces, please. I need to make a very important phone call." And with that, Mum headed to the hallway feeling an enormous sensation of positivity and belief that something very important had happened today, and hopefully changed their lives for the better.

Chapter 12

Pause for thought

Chika Change-Your-Thoughts wriggled with glee at how everyone involved in this project was working really hard to make the right changes for Robbie and also for themselves.

Cale had taken their chat very seriously. He entered the interview room feeling like he had been dared by Chika Change-Your-Thoughts to do something different. One thing Cale thrived on was a challenge. Several times throughout the meeting Cale felt his brain craving to do things as before.

He wanted to challenge the Officers asking him the same old questions. He desperately wanted to channel all the frustration and anger he was feeling and direct it at them to make himself feel better. But each time he did, the wise words of Chika Change-Your-Thoughts popped into his head and steered his thinking towards staying calm, not only for himself but also to set an example to Robbie.

The officers in charge of the interview looked confused with this different attitude that Cale was presenting. Cale was so well known in the local police station that the on duty staff used to take turns in who was to interview him next! The Officers also recognised that, most times with Cale, it was his attitude that got him into the most serious trouble, not necessarily the low-level acts that he was involved with.

As the time ticked away, Cale started to surrender to his negative thinking and feelings. “Why aren’t you listening to me? I never held the kid against his will, and I never laid a finger on him. He was upset, kicking the living daylights out of a load of tin cans at the top end. He was being so loud it stopped me from my tinkering. WHY AREN’T YOU LISTENING TO ME?”

Cale raised his hands in anger and was just about to slam them down on the table when a knock on the interview room door interrupted the flow.

“Can I have a word, PC Samad? I have some important information that I think you should know about with regard to this incident,” said PC Hallatt.

“Right Cale, you can have a five-minute breather. This might be the last one you get for a while. Have a walk around, as you young man could be here for some time,” said PC Samad sternly.

Cale screeched the chair legs across the floor as he stood up. His brain was flooded with all kinds of things. Never had an interview been suspended for the addition of further information. Maybe this was more serious than he thought. He paced around the room fearful that Chika Change-Your-Thoughts help was not going to work. As he faced the wall, staring up at the tiny window, Chika Change-Your-Thoughts appeared.

"I never said this was going to be easy, Cale. Doing things differently is difficult, but just because it is tough doesn't mean that you stop trying; it's when you try *harder.* You can do this," whispered Chika Change-Your-Thoughts.

"I didn't think it would be this tough. They've already made up their minds. Some other information has come in to pin on me. It's too late. I've learned all this too late," whispered Cale, feeling hopeless.

"Since when were you a mind reader?" said Chika Change-Your-Thoughts.

"You're giving up on the situation based on things that you think are going to happen.

Stop letting your imagination take you into negative thoughts. Bring yourself back to the present and do what you need to do. You can do it!" Chika Change-Your-Thoughts disappeared just as the door creaked open and PC Samad returned.

"Please come and sit down, Cale. It appears that what you were telling us was the truth. We've just had a phone call from Robbie's Mum explaining what happened, earlier today at the garages. She even wanted me to pass on her and Robbie's thanks, as apparently you were a great help. You even got him to face up to what he had done and to do the right thing," said PC Samad.

Cale breathed a huge sigh of relief. Maybe doing little things differently did make the outcome better.

His thoughts were suddenly bombarded with police interviews from the past. So many of them had ended up with him losing his temper and spending a night in a cell, regardless of whether he had or hadn't done the said deed.

He could have been doing the same tonight if he had not taken Chika Change-Your-Thoughts advice. Not even a phone call from Robbie's Mum could have saved him from that. However, a change in attitude and a Cale supporter could have some impact.

"So, Cale, it seems like you might be turning over a new leaf. Not sure what happened with you today, but whatever it was, keep it up. Or whoever has been talking some sense into you, keep listening to them. They know what they're talking about," said PC Samad reassuringly.

Chika Change-Your-Thoughts glowed from behind the recording device on the table.

Cale beamed too. "Thanks, erm... yeah, erm, really thanks." He was in shock but pleased with how the day had turned out.

"You keep this up, Cale, and you could be a real help to us down here at the station. We are always on the lookout for people who can share their mistakes and experiences with younger kids, who might be heading on the wrong path. I was impressed with you today. You did well. Now get on your way," said PC Samad, with a genuine smile.

Cale left the station feeling like he had spent the last few hours in a dream.

How come he hadn't realised before all the things he had learned today? Why hadn't anyone cared enough to share this information with him when he was little? He knew the answer to that already, because he didn't care and wouldn't have listened.

Would the kids that PC Samad was talking about listen to him?

Chika Change-Your-Thoughts plonked herself on the inner crease of Cale's elbow. "See, I know what I am talking about." She gave him a cheeky smile. "*You* did all the hard work; you could have ignored it and done things exactly as before, but you made a good choice today and guess what...? I think today could be the start of many more good days!"

"I can't believe that I woke up this morning feeling the same doom and gloom about my life and my future. Yet two relatively small changes have had such a huge effect on how I feel. It's like I've won the lottery," said Cale.

"You have. Positive feelings are worth so much more than money. Now hold on to them somewhere special inside, to always remind you about how great you can feel. If you don't look after and appreciate these precious emotions of happiness, pride and hope they will fade away," said Chika Change-Your-Thoughts seriously.

"Thanks, Chika Change-Your-Thoughts. Thank you very much. I feel I need to thank Robbie too. He introduced a side of me today that I never knew I had. Maybe I should pop to his house and thank his Mum for what she did too."

"That would be a lovely idea, Cale. But go home and sleep on it, you've all had an eventful day. Maybe you could go when you've had time to think about what you've learned from today and what you would like to say. It also offers something good to do on another day to keep these feelings alive," suggested Chika Change-

Your-Thoughts.

"Yes, good idea. I'm just scared that this lovely feeling will go and I'll never get it again," said Cale.

"You've made a payment into your feel good bank today, Cale. The way to stop it disappearing is to keep doing good things that make you feel good. Then your account will stay topped up. You have lots of goodness in you, but you must share it," explained Chika Change-Your-Thoughts.

"Yes, you're right. I'm going to thank Robbie and his Mum and I'm going to use my disaster of a life to help all the kids who could end up like me. I can show them that I understand them and try and help them find better ways of doing things," said Cale.

Cale and Chika Change-Your-Thoughts high-fived a successful partnership and a very productive day. Without realising it Cale, like Mrs Tucker, was helping Robbie change his anger.

But Chika Change-Your-Thoughts knew that it was Robbie who could do the most to manage his anger and over the next few weeks they were going to get to know each other very well; very well indeed.

Chapter 13

Nose jewels

Over the short period of time that Chika Change-Your-Thoughts had been involved with Robbie, she had noticed lots of patterns to Robbie's anger. She recognised that Robbie was much more easily angered when he was tired and hungry, as we all can be, but this one could easily be changed.

The more difficult issues, like with Cale, was changing some of the bad habits that they had both learned from how others, within their family, displayed and managed their anger in the past. On top of that, for Robbie, was the grief his family were still struggling with, and how it had made them unhappy over the last few years.

Chika Change-Your-Thoughts felt that she had gained a good understanding of Robbie and his anger issues. However, she knew that it was no use whatsoever having this information unless she shared it with Robbie, so that he understood it too. The last few days had been emotionally exhausting for Robbie, so she decided to leave it a couple of days, but watch carefully to see how the changes with Mum affected how Robbie was feeling.

As the night time quickly arrived, Chika Change-Your-Thoughts decided that she would head over to the midnight meeting slightly earlier than normal. Not only did she want to see all her friends and share the happenings of the day, she also wanted to see if The Blinks communication switchboard could help her with a possible plan that she was crafting.

The Blinks had only developed this ability to manipulate technologies over the last few years. Many Blinks had amusing stories of travelling along telephone wires as highly static fluff, or accidently popping up on TV screens in the middle of adventure films or soap operas!

Blink 21869 Sophie Set-Goals remembers only too well the days before such electrical devices and how much simpler things were then. She remembered not too long ago Blink 211101 Leila Love-Who-You Are asking for information on 'iPads'. Poor Sophie Set-Goals spent fifteen minutes talking about how gauze was much better as an 'eye pad' for an 'eye' injury than cotton wool due to it not being so fluffy!

Chika Change-Your-Thoughts decided that, after what had been a very eventful day, she would spend a few hours in the bakery pondering over the next stages of her project. When she arrived, the shop was deadly quiet and only partially lit by the glow of the moon and a flickering street light.

As Chika Change-Your-Thoughts was tiptoeing around the room searching for somewhere to sit, she was suddenly startled by scurrying and scratching noises. Chika Change-Your-Thoughts was convinced that she would be here on her own. This noise couldn't have been from another Blink as there was no gentle glow in which to be recognised. It was unlikely to be a human either, as Rosie the baker would have left hours ago.

Suddenly, she heard the scurrying again, but this time it sounded more distressed and frantic. Chika Change-Your-Thoughts decided to follow the sound, which appeared to be coming from the washer room at the back of the shop.

Chika Change-Your-Thoughts had never been in there before, and it was very dark.

Once she felt it was safe and human free, Chika Change-Your-Thoughts increased her glow to the maximum to try and see what was making the noise.

Chika Change-Your-Thoughts saw the washing machine first. On the floor was a basket, containing several of Rosie's white bakery coats waiting to be washed. She noticed the sink above. Then a shelf with neatly folded tea-towels and what looked like a year's supply of cleaning products. But what had made the noise that she had heard earlier?

As Chika Change-Your-Thoughts continued to investigate, the noise happened again. This time, it was close by. She tuned in her excellent hearing and followed the frantic scratching.

Chika Change-Your-Thoughts was getting closer and closer to the floor and closer and closer to the laundry basket. She then noticed that the sound and the movement were coming from what looked like the pocket of one of Rosie's coats. As she moved closer, Chika Change-Your-Thoughts saw a young mouse, obviously in some form of discomfort.

On closer inspection, Chika Change-Your-Thoughts saw that the tiny mouse had something stuck on the end of its nose. The mouse initially looked scared of her, but was soon put at rest when Chika Change-Your-Thoughts gave off her calming, safe vibe.

"It's okay little mouse, you look like you're in some pain there. If you let me help you, I can remove whatever that is on your nose," reassured Chika Change-Your-Thoughts.

The mouse quickly stopped wriggling which gave Chika Change-Your-Thoughts the confidence to help more. As she approached the mouse, she recognised instantly what was lodged on its nose. It was small and red, with holes just big enough for a curious mouse to get his nose tip jammed in to, with no way of removing it.

With a gentle wiggle and a quick tug, the button loosened and the mouse was free at last. If mice could smile or show their appreciation, then the cute youngster definitely beamed gratefulness. It then scurried under the gap of the outside door and was gone.

Chika Change-Your-Thoughts felt doubly happy. One happy mouse and a lovely surprise for Peter Practise at tonight's meeting. Chika Change-Your-Thoughts could now do what she had intended when she first arrived; have some rest and reflection.

Several hours later the bakery was buzzing with positive energy from The Blinks population, all excitedly sharing their passions from the day. Chika Change-Your-Thoughts had been desperate for Peter Practise to arrive so that she could give him his special button back. Just as Chief Blink was about to silence the giddy assembly in came Peter Practise looking scruffier than normal.

Chika Change-Your-Thoughts knew that now wasn't the time, but as soon as everyone headed for their meeting place she would reunite Peter Practise with his button. Chief Blink did not keep The Blinks long but, as usual, shared her eternal gratitude at the good work of The Blinks, and then told a story with a positive moral; tonight's being about not giving up when things are difficult, but to try harder.

Robbie and Cale both came into Chika

Change-Your-Thoughts' head at this point. How true was that moral going to be if either of them wanted to make changes for the better. She also noticed Peter Practise nodding wholeheartedly which was perhaps in support of his determination to find his beloved button.

While The Blinks moved to their various places around the bakery, Chika Change-Your-Thoughts headed straight for Peter Practise.

"Hi, Chika Change-Your-Thoughts. How are you today?" said Peter Practise. But he never gave her a second to answer. Instead, he launched straight into the frustrations of his day. "I have not stopped looking for my button and I still haven't found it. I even slipped down a plug hole which would never have happened if my button had been attached. That is why I look a bit of a mess. It was wet and awful down there. Yuk! Do I smell?"

Chika Change-Your-Thoughts had

caught a slight whiff, now that he had mentioned it "Mmm, maybe slightly. It might be worth your while popping over to the grooming section tonight, so that you can smarten yourself up a bit; especially now that you can add this to your Blink outfit." With that Chika, Change-Your-Thoughts held out her hand and showed Peter Practise his beloved red button.

Peter Practise gasped with so much joy that the room fell silent for a split second, but very quickly got back on track. "Thank you so much, Chika Change-Your-Thoughts. How? When? Where?"

For quite a while, the story of the baby mouse entertained Peter Practise and several other Blinks who had become interested since hearing the 'gasp'. Chika Change-Your-Thoughts then politely explained that she needed to head to The Blink switchboard for some technological information that was to be crucial to Robbie's project.

Peter Practise also wanted to make sure that he left the meeting tonight with his wonderful red button in one place only; back where it belonged on the end of his sunshine yellow hat. Tonight the midnight meeting proved to be a success all round, which made tomorrow an exciting new day.

Chapter 14

Action!

Over the remaining week, Robbie started to feel less angry and less often. Though, his bad habits and his super quick reactions, when something didn't go as he wanted it to, were still causing problems at home and school.

One day, Robbie accidentally trapped Charlie's finger in the door frame, after getting cross at him for always wanting to play. There was also another day at school when his old bad habits crept back in; Tim, a boy on his table, commented that he had spelt a word wrong. Poor Tim genuinely didn't mean to cause any offence. In fact, Tim and his twin sister Bladen were two of the gentlest children in the whole class.

Tim had always been secretly envious of Robbie and how his expression of his feelings was so honest. Tim and his sister had zero self-confidence and this had affected them all their life.

Many times, Tim and Bladen had chats about how they wished they could sometimes show negative feelings. However, they were too scared to, in case they got told off or rejected. Their self-esteem was so low that they spent most of their day trying to make people like them. So the day when Tim tried to make Robbie like him it could not have gone more wrong.

What Tim hadn't realised was that Robbie was very sensitive to criticism. He saw it as people thinking he was stupid or a failure. This is why Robbie got angry. Tim had tapped into one of Robbie's beliefs about himself, that he *was* a failure!

This activated Robbie's internal volcano. Suddenly his mind was flooded with negative thoughts about himself, about life and about poor old Tim. Robbie ripped the page out of his book, rolled it up into a ball and threw it at Tim's head. Robbie felt dreadful within seconds of doing it, and could not apologise enough to Tim.

Tim could see straight away that Robbie was sorry and so decided not to tell. Robbie was really grateful for this and it made him think that Tim was actually a pretty sound kid.

"You're actually alright you, Tim. I always thought you were a bit wimpy. But what you did there was strong, you accepted my apology without telling. Not sure I would have done that. You're cool, so thanks. Do you want to do diablo tricks at lunch time?" said Robbie.

Nobody had said anything like that to Tim before. He knew he was a wimp really and part of the reason that he didn't tell on Robbie was that he really couldn't handle any confrontation. However, he could see that Robbie hadn't realised that, so that was good.

"Yes, that would be ace," replied Tim proudly.

Chika Change-Your-Thoughts had witnessed these many events and knew that stage two was needed as soon as possible. Robbie was not able to make the changes he needed on his own, he definitely needed her help.

Later that evening, Robbie was sprawled on the settee with his electronic tablet. While he was half watching the television and half playing a crazy Japanese game that involved him slicing up fruit, something suddenly appeared on the tablet's screen. There, looking directly at him, and surrounded by melons, bananas and pears was a purple fruit with human features.

Robbie tried to slice the unusual looking object as if it were part of the game.

"Hey, don't do that, it might hurt me. I'm not part of the game, Robbie. I am Blink 1970 Chika Change-Your-Thoughts and my job is to help kids like you who are not having a great time in life," she said.

Robbie did what most humans do when a Blink becomes visible for the first time, the double blink gulp!

"No, you're not imagining me. You might be a bit surprised that I've popped up on your screen, but very soon you will realise that I've been very close to you over the last few weeks, and I've been championing your cause. I know all about your Dad, the tough few years you've been having as a family, the unhappiness your Mum has been dealing with, the pencil shavings and Cale," said Chika Change-Your-Thoughts.

"But how can you know all that?" asked Robbie.

"I am a Blink. We're around all the time, looking out for kids having difficulties in their lives. You have become very interesting to me, so here I am," explained Chika Change-Your-Thoughts.

"If I seem interesting to you now, you should have seen me a few weeks ago. I was top news! Hang on, it sounds as if you did, if you know about the nightmare day when I met Cale," said Robbie.

"Yes, I do. My energies were drawn to you while you were in the garage with Cale. I was actually sitting on the garage door!" giggled Chika Change-Your-Thoughts.

"So why are you here? What exactly are you? Are you a cartoon character?" whispered Robbie, suddenly conscious that he was talking to a screen.

"I'm here because we need to do some work together. I'm going to help you understand what is going on with your anger. Then we're going to set little challenges so you can learn to do things differently.

"You know that your anger is a problem sometimes, it's because it seems that it's in charge of you. You are in control of your anger Robbie, not your anger in control of you," said Chika Change-Your-Thoughts. "Oh and I'm not a cartoon character. Would you like me to become real?"

"Yeah, that would be cool," said Robbie.

In a flash, Robbie's screen came to life again and started throwing random pieces of fruit upwards ready to be sliced. Chika Change-Your-Thoughts was perched on the top of it.

"This is awesome," said Robbie, just as the living room door swung open. Robbie quickly grabbed Chika Change-Your-Thoughts and popped her in his mouth.

"Who are you talking to, Robbie?" asked a suspicious looking Beth.

"Erm mo-one itsh djust the game." Robbie's garble made very little sense at all with a mouth full of Chika Change-Your-Thoughts.

"What are you eating?" asked Beth.

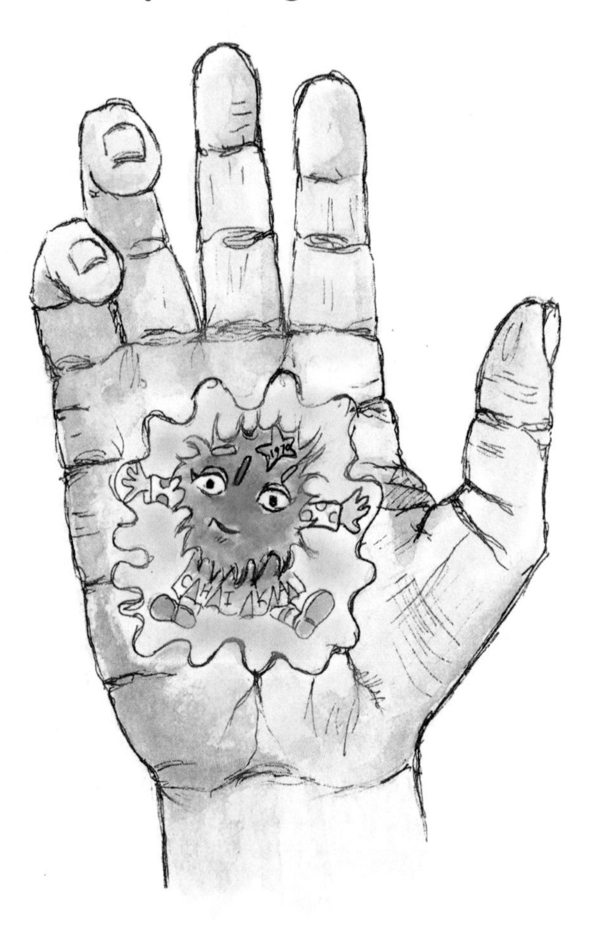

"Mothing, I am djudt twying to annoy you," said Robbie, hoping this would work as well as it usually did.

"Humph, you are sooo annoying. I'm going." And with that, Beth left in a strop.

A quick check that the door had shut, and Robbie gently spat in to his hand a soggy Chika Change-Your-Thoughts.

"Well, my job is to get to know you, but I normally work with the mind, not with the tonsils!" laughed Chika Change-Your-Thoughts.

This made Robbie chuckle too.

"So should we get started on changing your anger, Robbie? This will only work if you want things to be different and you are prepared to put in some effort and action. You will get homework," said Chika Change-Your-Thoughts.

Robbie's shoulders dropped. "I hate homework."

"This isn't normal homework. It involves thinking and doing rather than reading and writing. The results are happiness and pride, not grades and levels," explained Chika Change-Your-Thoughts.

"Sounds okay, I suppose. Yes, I'm in," said Robbie.

Over the next hour, Chika Change-Your-Thoughts shared all her knowledge and understanding of the anger emotion with Robbie. Her first thing was to take the bad feeling away. She explained that anger isn't the bad guy; it's what we do with anger that becomes the problem.

Robbie liked this. He always felt like he was a bad person because he did bad things when he was angry. He also welcomed the idea that people and situations do not make us angry, they only awaken our angry feelings. We are solely responsible for how angry we let these situations make us.

Chika Change-Your-Thoughts was really

impressed with Robbie and how hard he worked to follow the important lesson on his anger. Together they were able to break down what had become a damaging part of who Robbie was, into more realistic chunks that just needed tweaking.

The biggest tweak was needed in Robbie's thoughts. If what Chika Change-Your-Thoughts was saying was right, this is where everything started going wrong.

They played a little game to help Robbie understand it.

"Okay Robbie, I want you to imagine that you have invited Amanda around to play. Amanda doesn't turn up, or reply when you message her to see where she is. What would you start to think?"

"Well, I would think she isn't my friend anymore, or she has gone out with someone else, or she is ignoring me or doesn't like me because I'm stupid," answered Robbie with alarming speed.

"Right, so straight away you have started thinking negative thoughts. How do these thoughts make you feel?" asked Chika Change-Your-Thoughts.

"Sad, lonely, fed up and angry," said Robbie.

"Exactly," declared Chika Change-Your-Thoughts. "So negative thoughts activate your anger volcano and make you feel negative. You need to think more realistically. You need to be an emotion detective. Where is the evidence that Amanda doesn't like you, thinks you are stupid or is ignoring you?"

Robbie thought for a while and couldn't think of anything he had ever done to Amanda to make her not want to be his friend.

"So we need your emotion detective to find other things that could be responsible for her not getting back to you, more factual evidence," said Chika Change-Your-Thoughts.

"Wow, I get it. Things like her phone might have been broken, maybe she forgot, maybe she was ill, perhaps they had to go somewhere in an emergency. I get it, I get it," shouted Robbie, putting his hand over his mouth so as not to draw more attention from his nosey little sister.

"How did these thoughts make you feel," asked Chika Change-Your-Thoughts.

"Calm, understanding, NOT ANGRY," half shouted Robbie, like he had just worked out the meaning of life!

Robbie and Chika Change-Your-Thoughts both did a little celebratory dance of delight at some great learning, but even better understanding. The next stage was for Robbie to put this learning into practise, and not let the negative thoughts drive his anger into becoming problem behaviour.

Robbie felt different. He felt like he understood himself better, and that maybe he wasn't the bad person that he thought he was. He was going to do this; and knowing that he had the support of his new friend, Chika Change-Your-Thoughts, he felt that this challenge was going to be one that he would not give up on.

Chapter 15

Chain reaction

Robbie became Chika Change-Your-Thoughts' star pupil. Over the following weeks, he took hold of his emotions and steered them in the right direction, which he had never thought was possible before.

Also, Robbie's anger detective became so efficient he was nearly promoted to Inspector! Robbie slowly began to realise that anger, like most emotions, comes and goes. More importantly he had lots of tools in his anger toolkit to help move it on as quickly as possible and reduce further damage.

Some days Robbie felt amazing, like he had cracked this negative emotion once and for all and was never going to feel angry again. Then other days his anger would slowly creep up on him and catch him unawares.

These days were the hardest for Robbie. He felt powerless, that he had reacted automatically in his old ways before he had a chance to even open his anger toolkit. Chika Change-Your-Thoughts knew this was a normal part of any change cycle, but what was the best way to get Robbie to understand it too?

It was on one of these difficult days, when Robbie was feeling particularly sad, that a surprise visitor decided to pop round to the Tucker home. Robbie heard the knock but was feeling far too sorry for himself to even switch from the low mood.

Through the gloom in his head, Robbie could hear Mum talking to someone in an upbeat tone. As the front door shut the conversation continued into the living room. Whoever it was had been invited in.

For some reason, Robbie felt intrigued by the visitor and strained to hear their voice. Again his mind was presented with the choices dilemma. Should he go down or stay upstairs? Mum actually made the choice very easy for Robbie when she shouted for him to come down, as someone was here to see him.

Who could it be? It couldn't be someone from school, it was a Saturday. It wouldn't be Amanda, as she had gone away for a family weekend. Curiosity flooded through him. He left his bedroom and headed downstairs towards the mystery guest.

As he got closer, he began to recognise the voice. As he opened the door, he was filled with warmth at seeing Cale again.

"Hey up mate, how are you? I was just passing and thought I would pop in and see how it's going. I also needed to say a huge thank you to you and your Mum for telling the police what really happened that day. I was really worried I was in big trouble," said Cale nervously.

"We did it because you were a real help to Robbie that day, we weren't going to see you wrongly accused of something you didn't do. Anyway, it's us who need to thank you. Do you want a cup of tea or a cold drink?" asked Mum, not sure if tea was too uncool for kids Cale's age.

"Tea would be great thanks, just milk please," answered Cale. "So how is it going then, Robbie? Did things turn out okay?"

"Yes, they did actually. Mum and I have become a lot closer and we've started talking more. She isn't as angry either, which is good. I've been trying really hard not to get as angry either, but I forgot everything earlier and threw a book at Vanessa, so now I feel rubbish."

"You're being a bit hard on yourself, aren't you? Okay, it wasn't the best choice but this is part of the journey. Its days like this when you do the most learning. Believe me, I have been on a rollercoaster since that day we met," said Cale.

"Why, what's happened?" asked Robbie, excitedly.

"Here are your tea and biscuits. I'm just going to hang the washing out and let you two have a chat. I won't be long," said Mum.

"Thanks, Mrs Tucker. Well, you know that day we met?" said Cale.

"Yes, yes," said Robbie, enthusiastically. He was so glad that Cale was here, helping him to change his gloomy mood.

"Well, you might not believe this, cos you didn't know me before, but I was not a nice person for a long time and so didn't do nice things. The more people didn't like me and thought I was trouble the more troublesome I became," said Cale, with his head hanging low. "It was watching you that day at the garages that woke a part of me up. I wanted to protect you from your life going the way mine had gone; I wanted to sort of save you."

Robbie didn't really know what to say. He noticed Cale's eyes were definitely more watery than when he started. "And you did. I didn't know what to do that day. I think if I hadn't met you, I would have hidden somewhere all day feeling angrier and angrier."

"Do you know what the funny thing is? As much as I wanted to save you, you actually saved me," said Cale.

Robbie couldn't hide his confusion at that comment. "Eh, I don't get it."

Just then Mum came back into the room. "All okay boys, do you want anything else?"

"No thanks', Mrs Tucker," said Cale. "But I would like you to hear what I'm about to say.

"The day I met Robbie changed my life. As you probably know, over the years, I've developed a bad reputation. Seeing Robbie so distressed made me want to help him, save him, but the thing is he saved me. It was like he unlocked a part of me I didn't know, a part that felt good. I hadn't felt that before.

"The great news is I don't want to lose it, so I've been working really hard not to get into trouble or go back to my old ways. The police have even said that if I can prove to them that I've turned over a new leaf then I can become a mentor, working with kids who are getting onto the wrong path."

Mrs Tucker was wiping tears from her eyes. "You're amazing, Cale. I'm truly proud of you for making such a huge decision to change what you're doing with your life."

"It's not easy," said Cale. "In fact, I have days like you're having today, Robbie.

My old ways creep back in too. It's hard when people still look at you with fear and disgust and cross the road when you approach them.

"Sometimes I want to shout and swear and barge them out of the way, because it hurts. Once or twice I have, but those times now make me feel sad and so they're getting less and less. If I can do it, Robbie, you can do it. It's all about practise."

"Yes we can," said Robbie. "We can do it together and help each other."

Mum was virtually blubbing now, tears of joy and pride oozing into her tissue. There were so many people that she knew in the area who she could tell this tale to. She was going to help Cale help Robbie, like a chain reaction of support.

Chika Change-Your-Thoughts, who was sat behind the picture frame on the mantelpiece, very rarely wept. However today, like Mum, she had become very moved by what had just happened and tracks of damp face fluff appeared across her cheeks.

She felt happy that this project was doing everything it needed to and she would be able to pull away in the not too distant future. Her Blinks intervention had glued three very special and important people together; ticking off rule number 1 of her intervention checklist.

What she hadn't realised was that both Cale and Robbie knew that she was there, as they had both been lucky enough to meet her and so sensed her presence. Yet neither of them had, or ever would, share The Blinks magic. It was too precious to lose. This was ace for Chika Change-Your-Thoughts as rule number 2 was also complete.

Chapter 16

Hope

As the months passed Robbie and Cale continued to move in the right direction. As expected, every now and then blips happened along the way. The difference now was:

- each of them had become better at learning the lesson when things went wrong
- they both had access to lots of new ways of doing things thanks to Chika Change-Your-Thoughts
- and more importantly they both had each other's support

These factors were the key ingredients to their success.

Cale became a mentor with the police force and helped many kids see the realities of their ways. Every now and then Cale slipped up and got too frustrated with a kid who he didn't feel was listening. On the odd occasion this happened, it appeared to work as the kids saw it as him really caring (which he did) and so all was good.

His reputation in the area changed with the majority of people. As can be expected, some folk won't let their minds be changed. Cale made the ones who still judged him, his challenge. He would use more effort to prove them wrong, and never again show them that they were right.

Cale and Robbie became lifelong friends and Cale became an honorary member of the Tucker family. They even helped him move from his damp, crumbling flat into one in a better part of town.

Robbie's successes included an award from Mrs Lomas for personal effort and growth. The award was given to him one Friday afternoon in the class celebration time. However, it wasn't Mrs Lomas who gave it to him.

His class teacher, Mrs Jackson, had also recognised the huge difference in Robbie over the last months and wanted to show Robbie that the past was the past. As she handed him the award, the class cheered and celebrated. Then one of his classmates handed over a white t-shirt which had been written on by everyone. On the front, it said, "What we like about Robbie...."

Everyone in Y6J had signed it, including Mrs Jackson. Robbie's cheeks glowed, and his smile stretched so much that it began to hurt. He was also nominated to be a peer mentor to help younger children who also struggled at times with angry emotions.

Another success was that Amanda had noticed too. "Robbie it's so wonderful to see you happier now. I still see you getting angry but you deal with it in a normal way now. People aren't nervous around you anymore."

"Were you scared of me, Amanda?"

asked Robbie nervously.

"Me, never! I was never scared of *you,* but I was scared of your anger sometimes," said Amanda honestly.

This conversation would add more to his feel good pot and keep reminding him of how anger affects other people too.

The greatest success for Robbie was how he felt about himself. He had challenged his feelings of failure and had now collected enough evidence that made questioning that belief much easier.

Many times Robbie wondered which came first. Today it was while he was doing his homework at the dining table. Did he feel less of a failure because he was less angry? Or was he less angry because he was less of a failure. Chika Change-Your-Thoughts decided to make one last visit.

"Hi, Robbie. How are you doing? Would you like some help in answering that question?" said Chika Change-Your-Thoughts.

"Chika Change-Your-Thoughts, wow, how are you? What question? Oh that question," said Robbie, slightly startled.

"I asked first," she said with a mischievous wink. "Anyway back to the question. You have worked really hard to develop your emotional understanding of anger, which helps you make better choices. Have you noticed that?"

"Yes, I have. I feel much more confident now that I quickly know what to do, so I get fewer things wrong," said Robbie.

"Exactly," cheered Chika Change-Your-Thoughts. "So that is the answer. The more we understand our emotions, the better we get at making right choices and that makes us feel stronger and more confident. The real word is resilient, which means our ability to cope with life's ups and downs."

"I get it. The more I get things wrong, the less resilient I become. Now that I'm making better choices I feel more resilient," said Robbie.

"Spot on Robbie, you have cracked the secret code! So what are your key tools in your anger toolkit; the things that work best for you?" said Chika Change-Your-Thoughts with great interest.

"My top anger tips are:

1) Challenge negative thoughts. Are they based on fact or what I think?

2) See the signs. I know that when I start to get angry I clench my fists. I now use this as a sign that I need to get my toolkit ready.

3) I distract myself (ignore it, walk away, breathe deeply, do something fun) whenever I can, so that I don't spend

too long thinking about being angry. This gives me time to let the angry feeling go.

4) I question what I can do. I ask myself 'What is making me angry and why?', 'Is this situation worth it?', 'What will happen if I do this now?' and 'What can do I differently, so that I'm in charge?'

5) I talk to my Mum, Cale and Mrs Lomas. If ever I feel my emotions are getting strong I know who to go to. This gets the difficult feelings out and also helps me understand them even more, and then I know what to do next time.

6) I will keep practising."

"Well haven't you become a wise one for your age?" said Chika Change-Your-Thoughts. There's only one more thing that you could add to your list. Don't be too hard on yourself when you get it wrong, and you will.

"Mistakes are a natural part of the change process. A failure isn't someone who gets things wrong, that is someone who is learning. I am over 200 years old, I think, and I'm still learning!"

"Wow, you're the oldest person I know, and I guess you have had lots of experience. So yes, what you just said becomes number seven on my list:

7) See getting things wrong as one step closer to getting things right."

Robbie and Chika Change-Your-Thoughts gave each other one last high five that they held for slightly longer than normal.

"Thank you, Robbie, for being a delight to work with. I have a very special place in my heart for this project. Look after yourself and look after your toolkit list."

"Thank *you*, Chika Change-Your-Thoughts. You will never know how grateful I am to you. You gave me hope that things could be better, and I now know that hope is worth more than gold," said Robbie, surprised at how clever some of his thinking had become.

"Goodbye," warbled Chika Change-Your-Thoughts.

Before Robbie had time to reply, she was gone. The dining room was still.

Robbie didn't feel the emptiness as a loss, though he was going to miss her. Instead, he saw it as a promotion. Chika Change-Your-Thoughts believed he was capable and ready to do this on his own, and no way was he going to let her or himself down.

As Robbie tried to take his mind back to his homework, he noticed a tiny yellow speck on his homework book. On closer inspection, it looked like a badge. As he picked it up he saw in tiny letters the words 'You are a special star -don't ever forget it', Chika Change-Your-Thoughts must have dropped it. Was it accidental, or had she left it as a small gift?

Nevertheless, whenever Robbie remembered those words, his anger weakened and his feel good factor stayed higher. So he made it his speech, which he repeated every day, more than once on tough days. The phrase gave him more hope and that made things feel better.

Chika Change-Your-Thoughts hadn't dropped it by accident at all, as you probably guessed. In fact, she made it especially for Robbie while she was having her seven days of wonderfulness. Popping back to answer the question was a great opportunity to leave it behind. She liked the phrase and felt that it summed up just what Robbie needed to be reminded of in the future. Maybe it is something that we all need to believe.

So as Chika Change-Your-Thoughts

would say "Try it. It might just help you too!"

The Blinks Reference Manual

Accompanying all the Blinks novels are Reference Manuals for parents, carers, older siblings, teachers and professionals. The supportive booklets provide a greater understanding of the psychology of all emotions and how they can impact on other developmental issues. They also provide lots of 'top tips' of what works best for children and young people whilst growing up and some activity questions that can be used as a starting point to initiate emotive dialogue or discussion.

Look out for The Blinks 3 - Self-esteem - due for release spring 2016.

Acknowledgements

This book as always comes with eternal thanks to my family and friends. For listening to my ideas, and supporting me on my journey in getting this book out there, you will never realise the real value of your role in this process.

In particular I need to say a huge thank you to my Auntie Karin, who at the stage of me writing this, is the only person on the planet who has read this book (3 times!) as my honorary and outstanding proof reader. Also thanks to Jill my official proof reader for her keen eye, especially with points of view! Also to Liz, a true Blinks Ambassador working hard to promote the books in Canada!

I would like to give a very special thank you to Lucy W who was the first child and human being to read The Blinks – Worry cover to cover within 24 hours of it being published, you are a star!

Thank you to my wonderful neighbours. In particular Fiona, Claire & Roop, for being so enthusiastic and refreshingly honest, when I needed it the most.

Also once again the amazing Rachel Pesterfield has brought the book to life with her awesome and vibrant illustrations, thank you Rachel your talent never ceases to amaze me.

Gail, my publisher and coach, I thank you for listening and encouraging me when I feel disheartened and sharing my excitement too, you are a star.

I would also like to thank *you*, the person who is reading this book right now. *You* are the one who I really need to thank as without *you* none of this would be happening. Thank *you* with all my heart.

Lastly I would just like to acknowledge the special people who the world has lost recently, but are hopefully sharing their love and wisdom within The Blink Universe; Mr Emmerson (my inspirational primary school teacher) and Nicky, from across the road.

About the Author

Andrea Chatten- MSc, MBPsS,

PGCL&M, Bed (Hons), Dip.CBT

Andrea Chatten has been a specialised teacher for over 25 years; working with children from ages 5-16 with emotional and behavioural difficulties. She is currently working as 'Lead Children's Emotional & Behavioural Psychologist' at Unravel CEBPC with schools and families in Sheffield.

Developing positive, trusting relationships has always been at the heart of her practice with children and young people in order to nudge them into improved psychological well-being. Over the years, Andrea has developed and applied many positive developmental psychology approaches.

This insight is incorporated into her stories in order to help children, young people and their families to gain more of an understanding and potential strategies to try, in order to deal with an array of behavioural issues that children and young people could experience.

Andrea created 'The Blinks' so that parents could also benefit from reading the books with their children; especially if they identify with the children in the stories, and their family circumstances. Both parent and child could learn how to manage early forms of psychological distress as a natural part of growing up rather than it become problematic when not addressed in its early stages.

The Blinks is a series of books that

discreetly apply lots of psychological theory throughout the story including Cognitive Behavioural Therapy, Developmental and Positive Psychology approaches.

This first book in the series tackles the issue of worry and how to prevent this everyday cognition from becoming more serious anxiety in the future.

www.unravelcebpc.co.uk

Facebook - /Theblinksbooks

Twitter - @BlinksThe

To order a copy of the first book in this series then please go to www.oodlebooks.com or Amazon.

Due to be released Spring 2016 is the third book in the series 'The Blinks – Self-Esteem'